The Five Flames Book 3

Lie The Liar

Kristina Circelli

A PERMUTED PRESS BOOK

ISBN: 978-1-68261-215-6
ISBN (eBook): 978-1-68261-216-3

Lie the Liar
The Five Flames Book Three
© 2016 by Kristina Circelli
All Rights Reserved

Cover art by Christian Bentulan

PERMUTED
PRESS

Permuted Press, LLC
permutedpress.com

Published in the United States of America

For all my favorite people who make up awesome stories for a living...
just don't go getting possessed by a demon.

The Five Flames Series

PROLOGUE

Savannah was calm, sleepy, as midnight swiftly approached. Shadows crept along sidewalks, traveling with the moon as it rose higher in the night sky, settling upon the house on Abercorn Street renowned for its bloody history.

On the outside, the home was quiet, peaceful even, as it stood against the inky void of night. On the inside, the atmosphere was thick with dark energy. It pulsed through the house, against the walls, building and growing until the Will O'Wisp all but shuddered every time it dared to wake.

They were angry, the three spirits that remained trapped within their fiery confines. Angry they lost the bids. Angry no others had dared to enter their tortured home. Angry they had not yet found a soul to host them for eternity. The Will O'Wisp fed off their anger, defeated by their presence yet infuriated by its imprisonment.

There had been none since Jason Waters. The city still teemed with gossip over the bloodbath that was Tessa Taylor, tour guides breathing out stories of the Taylor Sibling Slaughters in ghostly monologues. A year following Tessa's descent into madness, Savannah still struggled to recover its reputation from the plague that began beneath its surface, devastating the city of Jacksonville and creating a hero out of one Jason Waters. Many illnesses had spread since the fateful RYF-2 outbreak, mutations of the Resurrected Yellow Fever virus that took the lives of innocent men, women, and children everywhere, and with every new mutation came a cure borne at the hands of a soul overcome by darkness.

Jason was a medical marvel, his demon giving him the credit and renown he'd always craved. Tessa Taylor was a feared killer, her demon transforming her into a woman strong enough to exact the revenge she'd always longed for.

There would be more, the Will O'Wisp knew. Three more to go through the bid. It always happened in a pattern; once the first demon secured its host, the rest soon followed in one way or another. The Will O'Wisp It could only wait for the moment one of those three would dare to enter.

A familiar voice brought the spirit out of the shadows, over to the window facing the main street. There, on the cracked sidewalk, stood the guide who had been part of the haunting since the beginning. The Will O'Wisp watched as the man gestured behind him, expression vivid, seeing the curiosity in his eyes. The guide had been looking upon the old house more frequently, perhaps wondering what had really happened to turn two otherwise normal human beings into monsters.

Soon, the Will O'Wisp told itself, the spirits flashing in rageful orange bursts. Soon the man would come back to them. Soon the bids would begin again.

CHAPTER 1

He stood at the corner, staring through the shadows at the crowd anxiously gathered at the Colonial Park cemetery entrance. A sigh built in his chest. Every night they gathered, waiting to hear stories of terror and mayhem, eager to discover what horrid secrets the sleepy Savannah town had to offer.

Not many secrets anymore, he considered as he began the slow trek down the cracked concrete on his midnight parade. His small city had been blasted across headlines in recent months, first just an off-hand comment about a murderess and her claims of possession, later an in-depth exposé questioning the safety of the very ground he now walked upon. He'd thought the negative press would keep people away out of fear. No, instead they came in droves with some sort of sick excitement for danger and intrigue.

Want to know all about the demons lurking in the night, he thought with a roll of his hooded eyes. They thought it was all a game, tales from a storybook written by an author with a wild imagination.

Think they know the truth about what lies beneath this city. Tourists flocking from all corners of the country, determined to debunk myths, curiosity piqued by the media and over-excited reporters.

All too eager to see if they can find the hidden meaning in a truth right in front of their eyes. The crowd turned at his approach, seeing the thin shadow stalking closer, set against a dark backdrop and starless night sky. They shifted, bouncing on foot to foot, lifting cameras and phones to document this momentous occasion upon which he would ask—

"Who wants to uncover all the dirty sins of Savannah?"

*

The crowd of ten grinned nervously at the sound of his deep, Irish-accented voice, glancing at one another in anticipation. They parted as he approached, then surrounded the man dressed in black, closing in to hear the introduction, whispered purely for effect.

"I am Augustus Jones, your fearless midnight leader into the city of ghosts. Welcome to Savannah, where sickness once spread through the veins of the earth, murders went unsolved for centuries, and hauntings are just a ghost tour away."

With that, he began the tour to the sound of tentative chuckles. "First things first, my brave companions. Everyone must check in. Otherwise, how are we to know who has been sucked into the underbelly of Savannah by the end of the tour?"

Pulling out a list from his back pocket, Augustus brushed back his thick, recently dyed black hair and began reading names. One by one the tourists checked in, the last name landing his gaze on a blonde-haired girl standing with her arms crossed and looking decidedly bored.

"Little adventurers must be thirteen or older," he said to the mother, who nodded.

"Hayden just turned thirteen," she replied. "My husband is here on business so we signed up for a tour for her birthday. I can show you her ID. We brought it just in case."

Before Augustus could hold up his hand, the woman brandished an ID showing the California seal and the girl's birthday. Thirteen, he noted, as of two days ago.

"Well, happy birthday, Miss Hayden," he said to the girl, who was nearly painfully thin, with porcelain skin and the brightest blue eyes he'd ever seen. She merely nodded and looked to the ground, mumbling a thanks.

Dismissing his young and grouchy tourist, knowing she would only be even surlier by the end of the night, Augustus flourished an arm decorated with a flared shirt and bangle bracelets toward the cemetery. "Shall we begin?"

He moved a few steps forward, through the bunched crowd, until he was standing on the steps leading into the cemetery. "We start our tour here, at the Colonial Park Cemetery. You may be wondering, why is this gate behind me locked?" He grabbed hold of the large padlock, ratting the chain wrapped around the metal gate. "This cemetery is home to many tragic stories, which we will uncover throughout our tour and when we return to this very spot, but even more recent tales of ritual and sacrifice. Imagine figures dressed all in black, lighting candles in the shape of pentagrams, slitting the throats of innocent goats and lambs as an offering to whatever demons they seek."

It was true. Some of it, anyway. "It doesn't look so good when the occult gathers in the cemetery at midnight, so officials closed it off. But, every now and then, someone slips in. Let us see if we can find a bloodied body on the other side of the bars."

His opening had captured their attention, as it always did. Sometimes he changed it up, telling the ghost stories upfront rather than at the end, but tonight his crowd seemed anxious and he knew exactly what they wanted to see.

Moving off the steps, Augustus led the group along the side of the cemetery, then down around the corner. He sucked in a deep breath, mentally preparing for the barrage of questions soon to come. They always came at two points in the tour, and this was the first one. Already he could see the questions and comments forming on the tip of their tongues, hands poised to raise if they couldn't get their words out before anyone else.

The crowd stopped in the middle of a clearing that butted up against the cemetery. Augustus waited until they were gathered to begin speaking. "I can see you all know where we are, but I'm going to make you wait for the good stuff."

He took a step forward, the toes of his boots touching the edges of a plaque that rose up from the outskirts of the verdant clearing. Not too long ago, he would have been standing on a cracked slab of concrete that used to be an old basketball court, and nothing more. Now it was a memorial. A living, breathing reminder of the death this city had caused.

"Once the city was cleaned up in the aftermath of the RYF-2 outbreak, officials decided to make this area a memorial, of sorts. The land had already been turned over and over by scientists and medical experts, the grass and dirt dug up and excavated, bones pulled from the earth to be studied. Hundreds of samples were taken and shipped to the most renowned labs across the world. Their goal was to figure out how the Resurrected Yellow Fever virus could have possibly survived underground, but their true purpose was to determine how it got out."

Isn't that the question on everyone's mind, he thought wryly. He could see that same curiosity on all of their faces. Except the newly minted teenager, who was determined to appear indifferent to everything he said.

Still not deterred from his tour, Augustus spread his arms wide. "The cities of Savannah and Jacksonville were razed, millions mourning the dead. But what would be left of this little corner of Savannah? New trees and flowers to symbolize growth, moving forward. A bench to allow visitors to reflect on the past and where they are in the present. And a stone plaque, so we will never forget the past."

Taking in a deep breath, he read the words etched into the plague. "*Celebrate the lives lived. Love the ones still living. Cherish the time given with all.* Lovely words written by Florida's own Jason Waters, to whom this very site is dedicated."

One of the tourists stepped forward, a lean older man with graying hair and circular glasses. "So this entire memorial here is named in honor of Jason Waters, the man who discovered the cure to the Resurrect Virus?"

"Yes." That was all he would say of the man named Jason Waters, unless otherwise questioned. And, Augustus knew, he would always be questioned. A year ago he welcomed the limelight, walked right into it whenever possible in hopes of finally claiming his lifetime of fame, but after Jason…nothing was the same.

"You know Mr. Waters, don't you?" the man continued.

Biting back a sigh, the guide nodded. "Yes, I do. Not personally, mind you. We met only briefly, during a rather exciting daytime tour where I walked him through our great city of Savannah as a personal escort."

A young woman stepped forward. Her hands clutched the strap of her purse. "Did you know him before the outbreak, or only after?"

"A bit of both, lass," he answered honestly. "We met after his hospital release to discuss Tessa Taylor, whom we will get to later on in the tour," he added when he saw several tourists about to jump on that tidbit. "It was around this time the virus was beginning to take hold. We went on a brief tour and then he went home. That was the last I saw of him."

The last time he thinks *he saw me, anyway.* Oh, but that was a truth Augustus would never share. He fought a shudder, remembering the night he tried so hard to forget, and refused to think of now.

"What do you think of him? Is he as much a hero as the news says he is?"

Augustus blew out a breath, keeping his gaze steady on the woman. "He's a good man," was his reply.

But a demon in disguise.

"He is incredibly intelligent, and used that intelligence for good. He saved a lot of people."

By first making them sick.

"He did something no one else could do when the Resurrect Virus struck. He healed them."

I just haven't figured out how the hell he did it.

And that was the crux of the issue, wasn't it?

Squaring his shoulders, Augustus half turned and gestured to the group. "Shall we?"

CHAPTER 2

Ever since Tessa Taylor showed up at one of his ghost tours, Augustus had rearranged his schedule to accommodate what had now become the highlight of the night. Everyone who signed up for a tour wanted to see one thing—the house of the alleged haunting.

He used to stroll by the house on Abercorn Street mid-tour, but now he made it their last stop before returning to Colonial Park Cemetery. Too many questions were asked that disrupted his flow. In the beginning, he'd loved answering them, craved the attention really, until the one question, *"Do you ever wish it happened to you, so you could tell real stories from first-hand experience?"* came, making Augustus realize they didn't care about him, just the thrill his stories could give them. Anyone who would actually think he wished he'd been possessed just for a story clearly didn't give two shits about him as a guide. He really was just entertainment, the hired help. And while Augustus was happy to earn a decent paycheck off their gullibility, his passion for the job had certainly waned over the last couple years...all because of the house on Abercorn.

The tourists gawked at the home now, some flashing cameras, others trying to peer in windows from the sidewalk. He let them go as far as the grass, keeping a watchful eye should anyone get too close.

"Some say, if you look closely enough, you can see a child in that front window, there." He pointed at one of the first-floor windows. "And sometimes a woman standing behind her. Ghosts of Savannah's past, forever trapped within those walls."

"Is it as evil as everyone says?" one of the women asked. There was a sadness to her voice, as though she pitied an inanimate dwelling over the dozens of lives lost within it.

Before answering, Augustus allowed his gaze to traverse the home for the first time that night. This was the house he'd come to love and hate. He'd made good money off his stories of the home's past, and what may have happened in its present. There were many speculations about Tessa Taylor's foray into the haunted house, and he played on them all, bringing in reporters and ghost hunters and tourists eager to uncover the truth.

And yet, the truth was he didn't know what happened, and didn't want to know. He'd been in that house before and vowed never to cross the threshold again. No, Augustus saw what Tessa Taylor turned into. What Jason Waters became.

Augustus Jones was no longer a skeptic.

"There's dark energy here," he finally answered the woman, who was now busy taking pictures and looking at them on her phone, likely searching for a ghost in the window. A scoff next to her had Augustus frowning and eyeing the teenager. "You don't believe me?"

"It's just a house," the girl earlier identified as Hayden replied. Her blue eyes rolled as she looked up at the house. "There's no such thing as ghosts. Everyone knows that."

"Don't mind her," Hayden's mother chimed in, snapping another picture. "She'd rather play those spaceship war video games than learn about history or current events."

Like most teenagers, Augustus mused, though he kept his expression stoic as he said, "Better be careful, little lass. Ghosts have a way of finding the ones who don't believe, and making the biggest believers of all out of them."

The girl rolled her eyes again. "Whatever," she muttered, pulling out her phone and starting to scroll through it, her attention no longer on the tour.

Shaking his head, Augustus focused again on the group. He gave them a few more minutes, answering various questions about Tessa and what he thought may have happened to her, before calling out to them. "All right, my brave explorers. This stop nearly concludes our evening's tour. I will now guide you back to Colonial Park Cemetery, where you will be regaled with the final stories of Savannah's past, and we will all go our separate ways."

He gestured toward the road, and the group gathered, falling into step behind him. One young man positioned himself at the front, asking Augustus questions as they began their return to the cemetery. "Is it true what they say about the Espy house? The stories about the gangster and all?"

Augustus started to give his opinion, but was interrupted by a panicked voice behind him asking, "Wait, where's Hayden?"

He paused mid-step, turning around to see that his group was, in fact, one person short. Before he could say anything, the girl's father chimed in, "It's been thirty seconds since we left that house. Where could she have gone?"

The others looked around, the mother starting to hyperventilate, but Augustus felt a rock drop in his gut. The situation felt all too familiar to one two years ago, when a worried fiancé noticed his betrothed and her best friend were no longer with the group.

Yes, he knew where Hayden could have gone. Where she *did* go. A snotty teenager who didn't believe in ghosts and thought the whole tour was stupid—of course she would go looking for trouble.

Hayden was in the house on Abercorn Street.

"Son of a bitch," he whispered. One hand dragged down his face and he knew, just *knew*, the only way she was coming out was if he went in.

Praying he was wrong, Augustus backtracked with the group, joining in as they called her name, her parents more insistently. A few of the tour members arced out on a side street, staying within view while searching for signs of the blonde-haired girl. When he came around to the front of the Abercorn house, Augustus dared to look up past the rounded staircase, eyes briefly closing on a resigned sigh at the sight of the slightly ajar front door.

"Ma'am," he called softly to Hayden's mother. She rushed to his side and he pointed, not surprised by her terrified gasp.

"What are we going to do?"

"I'll get her," Hayden's father replied, anger clear in his tone. "Hayden! Get out here right now!"

Augustus waved him off his stomach churned. "Sir, I can't allow you to trespass, and shouting will only disturb the neighbors. I will go in and get her. Better for me to go since I know the area and residents better."

The other man agreed after a moment's hesitation, stepping back and sliding an arm around his wife. The rest of the group surrounded them, a few of the women offering murmured comforts and reassurances to the parents.

Shaking his head, hating himself for doing what he swore he'd never do again, Augustus stood on the cracked concrete step, one hand on the cold metal railing as he stared at the front door, the small sliver of black seeming to mock his cowardice. Behind him, the crowd of tourists huddled together, some looking annoyed with the disruption, her parents an equal mix of worried and furious. The father continued calling the teenager every ten seconds, only to be redirected to voicemail every time.

Just wait until I get a hold of her, Augustus thought grimly, not at all pleased he now had to go retrieve her. It was a liability to let anyone else go in the house; he was risking his own job as it was. But it was more than that. This house.... It had a presence. A history. A darkness he could feel seeping through the crack in the open door.

That was Augustus's first inclination that something was wrong. This door was always locked. Police and town officials made sure of it, after news broke of Tessa Taylor. The fact that it was unlocked, allowing the teenager to enter, was a foreboding enough sign.

Someone—something—wanted a visitor.

Steeling his nerves, Augustus forced a façade of courage and pushed the door open, shining his flashlight around the foyer. He'd only seen the inside of the house once, but remembered it well. The narrow, steep staircase leading to a shadowed second story. The dirt and garbage-strewn floors. Furniture covered with dusty sheets that used to be white but were now a dingy yellow. A mantle place with old pictures, and a few selfies of brave—if not foolish—tourists.

And, worst of all, the oppressive feeling of evil causing his skin to tingle.

Augustus took in a deep breath. "Hayden?" His voice came out quieter than he'd intended, which irritated him. He might have been scared of the house, but hell if he would let some punk kid know it.

"I don't have time for this, kid. You have about five seconds to get your ass to the front door." *Much better*, he told himself when he heard the fierceness of his tone.

The seconds passed. Silence met his ears, his demand ignored. Sighing, Augustus took a few steps forward, remembering the last time he'd been in this house. It had been a mistake to bring Jason Waters here. He should have known the man would want to go inside, despite barely being able to walk at the time. That visit had been fine, creepy, but still fine, until he came across Jason standing in the hall.

He remembered it now as his feet led him through the living room, flashlight sweeping over antique furniture. The dark hallway, a gaping hole that seemed to swallow light, and Jason standing at the end, staring at the wall. There'd been a blankness to his expression, almost sleepy, completely disconnected to the outside world.

Augustus had called his name, over and over again, not wanting to go down the hall, eventually sneaking along the wall until he could grab Jason by the arm. Even then, it took several minutes to render the other man conscious, just to have Jason insist only a few seconds had passed.

At the time, Augustus didn't think much of it, attributing Jason's confusion to exhaustion, maybe some leftover pain meds, or simply hallucinations brought on by the trauma of his attack. Then the plague happened, and Jason Waters, former lab director turned medical expert extraordinaire, became king of the world. Augustus didn't know exactly what happened in this house, but he knew it all had to be connected.

"Hayden!" he called again, focusing on the girl rather than memories of his last visit in the house. Yet it was those memories that pulled him toward the same hallway where he'd found Jason. As he approached Augustus held his breath, hoping, praying, silently begging the girl wouldn't be there. At this point he'd rather her be outside laughing at the stupid tour guide who thought she was still inside.

"Shit." The single word escaped on a chilled breath when he saw her, standing straight as a board and staring into the inky black hole of the hallway. Even his flashlight couldn't penetrate the oppressive shadows. Slowly he crept down the hallway, searching his sides for signs of anything out of the ordinary, but there was only Hayden and her eerie silence.

"This isn't funny, kid. You need to leave with me, right now."

Hayden turned to look at him, her eyes large and round. "I like it here. You can't tell me what to do."

"Want to bet? Let's go," he ordered when he finally reached her, tempted to grab her by the arm but worried her parents might freak out of he touched their daughter. So instead he held out a hand and pointed where to go. After a moment of sulking, she complied, then paused in step.

"What's that?"

"I don't have time for your games."

"No, really. Look," Hayden insisted. Her blue eyes widened, and in them Augustus saw the slightest hint of fear. "What…what are those lights?"

His heart pounded as he followed her gaze, seeing three floating lights down the dark hallway. The same dark hallway Jason fell into his hypnotized state, he added as his stomach began to ache with dread. And then, before he could stop her, Hayden was gone from his side and starting toward the flames.

"Hayden!" Augustus reached for her, but she was moving quickly. Instinct had him moving as well, rushing to catch up with her. His hand touched her wrist the moment she stopped, and he looked up to see the lights were right in front of them. Flickering. Burning.

Inviting.

He felt sleepy, confused, barely alert enough to mumble as a feeling of complete abandon overtook him, "Hayden, we have to…."

CHAPTER 3

"Go."

The word finished his sentence, one he didn't remember starting. Augustus blinked a few times, feeling like cobwebs in his head were slowly breaking apart, allowing in clarity and rational thought. Realizing he was holding the girl's wrist, he let her go, wondering when he'd grabbed her in the first place, and what the hell he was doing in this godforsaken hallway.

"...Go?"

The sleepy voice had Augustus shining his flashlight on Hayden, who looked like she'd just woken from a deep sleep. Shit. He knew that look. Jason Waters had that same expression when Augustus found him in the hallway. And after....

Shit, he thought again. Hayden wasn't the only one in the hallway. She wasn't the only one who felt sleepy. *No*, he continued internally, *I've been here once and was fine. It's all in my head. We just need to get the hell out of here.*

"Yes," he said out loud to the teenager. "We have to go. Your parents are worried."

This time, she didn't protest. Hayden fell into step next to him and together they fled the house, Augustus yanking the door shut behind him. At the sidewalk, Hayden allowed her mother to pull her into a hug, while her father lectured her on such stupid and irresponsible behavior.

Augustus watched them for a moment, then shook his head, struggling to get back into his tour guide persona. He forced a suave smirk and puffed out his chest a bit for added effect. "All right, my weary travelers, how's that for some excitement at the end of a ghost tour?" He grinned a grin he didn't really feel, but it was enough to have his tourists chuckling. "Let's head back to the cemetery and conclude our tour for this fine midnight eve."

The group turned and began the walk back. Augustus held out a hand to Hayden's father, motioning for him to pause. "How long were we in there?" he quietly asked the man, who shrugged.

"Five, six minutes, maybe?" he guessed, then shook his head. "I'm really sorry about this. She can be a good kid, when she's not hell bent on being a pain in the ass."

"Teenagers," Augustus offered with a strained laugh, then led the man, his family, and a collective of strangers home.

*

From the window it watched, saddened by the heartache soon to befall the people and yet overjoyed that two had entered instead of one. Two who were susceptible to influence. Two who had succumbed to darkness, all while believing they still walked in the light.

The spirits were angry, angrier than they'd ever been before, and their fury gave them power. It gave them the strength to take these two at once, to enter into the bid and claim their souls. The one the Will O' Wisp had seen once before had made a foolish mistake, daring to enter the house of the five flames for a second time.

Augustus had been lucky the first time, appearing when the bid had already started, his soul not quite ready to be taken. But now time had passed. His life, his actions, his longings, were different, and no matter how hard he tried to stay away, the demon found him anyway.

The Will O'Wisp wanted to mourn for this man and child, as it had mourned for Tessa and Jason. But, this time, it was almost happy. For now only one flame remained, burning atop its hand. The brightest flame. The angriest spirit.

One remained, waiting to be freed. And when it was, the entire world would suffer.

CHAPTER 4

There was a chill in the air when Augustus finally entered his two-room, bungalow-style home. Temperatures were rapidly dropping this time of year, reminding him he still needed to fix some of the window seals and figure out where that annoying draft was coming from in the living room.

He'd lived in this house for twenty years, grew up in it as his second home. Back then, it was been a nice enough place. Small, but plenty of room for him and his mother, with all the comforts they needed. Now it was falling apart. Time hadn't been kind to the house, repair demands building up with each passing year, and not enough money to go around to fix them all. His job as a ghost tour guide, while entertaining, had never been profitable enough to warrant significant updates, and after his mother retired, funds got even tighter.

Worry about the house later, he told himself as he headed for the kitchen to grab a beer before falling into bed. In the kitchen, he ignored the dishes piled next to the sink, the trash needing to be taken out, pretending his life was significant enough to deserve a maid who would come by first thing in the morning to take care of it all.

"Why should I have to do it all?" he grumbled beneath his breath, yanking a cold beer off the shelf.

A creak behind him had Augustus biting back a sigh. He was tired, and didn't feel like a two AM recap of his night. Still, he turned and smiled at the elderly woman standing in the kitchen doorway.

"Did I wake you?" he asked his mother, who waved a gnarled hand at him as she entered slowly, feet shuffling across the floor to the small, cracked counter. She wore a thick pink nightgown that had seen better days, her long gray hair tied back in a messy braid. When she looked up at him, it was with a warm smile and kind blue eyes that defied the years they had seen.

"You know I never sleep long," she replied, and he knew it was the truth. His mother was plagued with rheumatoid arthritis pains and a failing bladder, which resulted in her waking several times throughout the night. Most days he marveled she was even able to get out of bed. "Tell me about your day."

"Can it wait until I get some sleep?"

"Oh," she waved another hand, "we are both awake now. What's a few more minutes? Besides, I'm an old lady, Nathaniel. I might not be here when you wake up."

"Mother," he replied, exasperated both by her dismal outlook and her use of his real name. She'd never once called him by his tour name, Augustus Jones, insisting he only go by the one she gave him at birth.

Still, there was some truth to her words. Gert Jones was an old woman, at times unhealthy, and very well might not have many years, months, days, left. So he resigned to the fact he would not find his bed for another hour and slid onto the stool next to his mother.

"There's my boy," Gert beamed up at him. One hand lifted to his face, a familiar gesture he'd known since he was a child by an affectionate and doting mother. "Such handsome, honest eyes," she murmured, peering into his dark eyes lined by thick black lashes. "Your grandfather's eyes. My daddy. He was such a good man. We should send him a Christmas card."

Gert paused, a frown creasing her face. "I mean…. Well, he would have loved a card, don't you think?"

The change in topic should have confused him, but Augustus was used to it by now. Her mind slipped a little more each week, and conversation wasn't always easy. So he simply nodded, not making a big deal out of her confusion. "He would have, Mom. And yes, he really was a good man."

"Yes." Her hand dropped to her lap. "Tell me, Augustus, how was your day? And none of that silly accent. You are my favorite little Colorado boy and that's the voice I want to hear."

Forcing a smile, Augustus recounted every part of his day, save for one part. He would never admit to entering that house on Abercorn Street. His mom was superstitious and always worried for his soul. Knowing he willingly went into an allegedly haunted house would have her up praying for him the rest of the night.

Only when he answered all her questions about the tourists and weather and critters that crossed his path at night was Augustus finally able to find his way to bed. He collapsed on top of the covers, instantly passing out.

Blind. He thought he was blind when he next opened his eyes. A suffocating blackness surrounded Augustus as he moved to sit up, only to realize he was already standing. Startled, he spun in a circle, panic starting to creep in when he realized he was no longer in his room, but was in…

A place he couldn't identify.

"What the hell?" he muttered, his skin prickling with a chill as it swept over him. "Anyone there?"

Silence greeted him. An almost painful silence, terrifying in its quiet. "Hello?" Augustus called again, just to hear something, anything, in this otherwise black void. He took a few steps forward, hoping he wasn't getting himself even more lost. But he had to move.

"Is...is this a dream?"

Idiot, he chastised himself. Of course it was a dream. Why else would he be standing in complete darkness when he knew for fact he just laid down to sleep?

And then, a glimmer of light in front of him. He reached out, needing to touch the only source of life in this place, but it flickered and startled him back a step. A voice came next, two voices—one young, one much older.

He instantly knew the older voice. The very sound of it caused his gut to churn and he wanted to look away, but his eyes were glued to the vision building in the air, which spun in a whirlwind of colors and hazy images. Soon it settled and he saw a scene he thought of far too often, the scene that made him what he was today—semi-famous around Savannah, but always one step away from where he truly wanted to be.

A little boy sat at a kitchen counter, water bottle clutched in both hands as he spoke into it. "Thank you so much for my award!" he boasted in a way only children could. Standing on a chair, he addressed the imaginary spectators before him, picturing them all smiling up at him and cheering his name. "I am so honored to get the award for best actor of the year! I'd like to thank my friends, and my mom, and—"

"Enough," a voice cut in, rough and bored and impatient all at once. The boy looked up, hurt evident in his big brown eyes, but he climbed down from the chair and set the bottle on the counter.

"Sorry," he whispered. "I was just practicing."

The man scoffed and yanked a beer from the fridge. "Practicing, eh? Ain't nothin' to practice for. You ain't never gonna leave this town and be one of them important people."

"I could," the child argued, his mind racing with all the possibilities the future had to offer. He could be rich! He could be famous! "Other people can do it, so maybe I can too."

The man slammed the beer down on the counter, the shock of the sound causing his son to jump. Pointing at the boy, he growled, "You listen, and you listen good. You ain't important enough to be famous. You ain't good enough to be in them movies. So get it out of your head that you can be something, and stop with those stupid dreams."

Then he turned and stalked away, leaving the little boy sitting at the counter, tears spilling down his cheeks.

"Son of a bitch," Augustus whispered, feeling a burn in his throat he swallowed back. Other words came to mind—*mother fucker, worthless sack of shit*—but he'd learned over the years to let them go. Resentment only served him so far.

"You always did think you were hot shit." So maybe he hadn't let it go after all. Augustus trained his eyes on the impossible floating vision in the air, watching his father stomp through the house, out the back door to his shed, where he'd drink a few beers and smoke whatever he could get his hands on. "No one else could possibly come close to the big and powerful Carter Jones. God forbid your kid turned out to be someone. Couldn't have that."

Bitterness continued to build the longer he watched the man. It didn't take long for his father to slump over in his tattered chair, and he remembered what happened on that day after he woke up. Another lecture, but this time complete with a fist swiped across a young Augustus's face.

"A complete waste of air," he muttered.

"A memory that still causes such fury," came a voice behind him. Augustus spun around, breath catching in his throat when he saw who—*what*—was standing behind him.

The woman, a ghastly creature with abnormally pale flesh, bright eyes, and flowing gown that made it look like she floated on air, edged closer to him. But it wasn't her skin or eyes that made his stomach clench in fear. It was her hair, and the coiling snakes wrapping around her head, nearly bringing him to his knees.

She stopped an arm's length away, staring at him with such intensity he felt like his insides were on fire. "Are…are you

Medusa?" he managed to ask, flinching when a low growl emanated from her throat.

"You humans are such an ignorant breed." But she didn't give him her name. Instead the woman circled around him, coming to a stop in front of the vision in the air, her body outlined in soft oranges and whites from the seventies-style décor of his childhood home.

"You hate him," she continued, unblinking eyes staring straight into his. The snakes slithered against one another to the tune of her voice. "So many years later, you hate the man who killed your dreams."

Augustus swallowed hard when she approached, lifting one beautifully manicured hand and stroking a finger down his cheek. He felt her touch deep in his body, craved it, yet at the same time was repulsed by it.

"You never had the chance to defend yourself," she crooned in his ear, "never were able to have your vengeance. I can give you what you crave."

The screen behind her changed then, shifting from a little boy in a kitchen to an adult Augustus standing over the body of an old man with a face far too recognizable. His father, staring up at him through wide, unseeing eyes, a gaping hole in his throat, likely caused by the gun tossed carelessly a few feet away.

"I can give you this," the woman continued, hands massaging his shoulders. "I can give you the revenge you want." Those hands moved lower, across his chest, sliding down his stomach as her soft chest pressed into his back. "I can give you vengeance that will make you feel whole again."

Augustus suspected he was supposed to feel some sort of sick satisfaction at the sight of his father dead at his feet. Instead he felt disgust, and confusion as to why this strange figment of his dream-state imagination thought it was what he wanted. Yes, he hated his father, but he'd never been one to sit around imagining different ways to kill people.

Turning away from the vision, he faced the snake-haired woman with as brave a face he could manage, achieving it only by telling himself this was all just a dream. "I learned a long time ago that hating my father to the point of wanting to kill him was pointless. The best revenge isn't death. It's my own success."

"Yes," she hissed, anger starting to take over seduction as her hands balled into fists, "but success has not been yours, because of the doubt he instilled. For that, you crave revenge."

"No, I don't," he argued. "I used to, but then I grew up. He's not to blame for my lack of success, or lack of anything. I am. And you, whoever you are, won't make me feel that kind of hate again."

He thought she would fight him, and was surprised when she retreated, a look of resigned disappointment mixed with an intriguing sort of sadness written in her expression. She appeared so distraught by his rejection that Augustus nearly called out to her to offer her comfort, before he too was pulled out of the darkness.

CHAPTER 5

Augustus shot up in bed with a hard gasp. Immediately his body turned this way and that, making sure he really was back in his bed. Moonlight shined in through the window, illuminating his familiar bedroom and drawing a sigh of relief out of him.

"What the hell was what?" he said, one hand rubbing at his chest. The dream felt so real; he could still feel the woman's hands on his shoulders, her fingers crawling all over him, pressing against his skin, reaching for all parts of him. Lower, lower still....

"You've got to be kidding me." All he could do was laugh at himself when he saw, or rather *felt*, the remnants of his dream and its effect on his body. "Shake it off, man."

Struggling to do just that, he threw back the covers and slipped on a robe, then stumbled to the single bathroom in his house, grunting in the harsh light after flicking the switch. One of the bulbs flickered, casting him in occasional shadows as he splashed water on his face. The cold helped wash away the dream.

With a sigh, Augustus shut the water off and stared at his reflection, noting how haggard he looked in the wake of such a strange vision. Not much time had passed, judging by the amazingly ugly bird-shaped clock his mother had hung in the bathroom years ago, but he felt like he'd spent hours in the dream.

The sound of dripping water pulled him from his reflection. "Piece of shit," he muttered down at the leaking sink, attempting to shut the water off and failing. A steady drip fell from the faucet, one he knew how to fix but would have to get the parts in the morning. "Everything in this fucking house is falling apart."

Frustrated, he turned away from the sink and returned to bed, trying not to think of all the things wrong with his old house, and how different his life might have been if he'd never experienced that painful scene in the kitchen as a little boy.

*

He rose early the next morning, unable to shake the effects of the snake-haired woman and her claim for vengeance. While he didn't think there was any hidden meaning to his mind fabricating her, surely something must be wrong for his brain to be bringing back such old memories.

Shuffling down the hall and into the small kitchen, Augustus greeted his mother with a kiss to the cheek. "Breakfast?" he asked, already heading to the fridge. It was routine after this long— scrambled eggs with cheddar, grits, and toast with strawberry jam. His mother's tastes never varied. It made it easier on him, never having to guess while ensuring she was eating properly, and taking her meds as the doctor ordered.

Gert settled her thin frame at the small table in the corner to watch her son cook. Once, she'd provided his every meal, and now he insisted on providing hers. "You are such a good cook, Nathaniel. You're going to make a woman so happy some day. Women love a man who can cook."

His back to his mother, Augustus rolled his eyes but replied, "We'll see, Mom. And it's Augustus, not Nathaniel."

"Not to me." Gert shook her head, gray curls bouncing around her head. "You'll always be my little Nate, even when you become a big star and no one knows your real name and everyone thinks you really do talk with that adorable Irish accent. And when you get a wife, I'll make sure she knows you're my little Nate too."

"If you say so."

When the food was ready, Augustus dished up two plates and set one down in front of his mother, then sat across from her. She ate slowly, as she always did, while he all but inhaled his food. Occasionally she would look up and smile, showing her appreciation. He offered the same smile back, though his was tinted with hesitation, his mind unable to let go of the dream, which he was now starting to think of as a nightmare.

Pushing the last bite of grits around his plate, Augustus debated voicing the concerns swimming about in his head. Finally he asked, "Mom...do you ever think about Dad?"

Gert stopped eating, setting her fork down slowly and dropping her hands to her lap. The change in her was instant and he regretted darkening the otherwise calm and soothing mood. "Why do you ask that, Nathaniel?"

He shrugged, not able to meet her eyes. "I had a weird dream last night. I guess it got me thinking about him. About the things he used to say to me."

Taking in a deep breath, Gert rose and rounded the table until she was next to her son. One hand lifted his chin to face her. "You listen to me, Nathaniel Jones. Your father was a bad man. We both know that. He was a bad man who said and did bad things, and the best thing that ever happened to us was him walking out and never looking back. I only wish I'd been strong enough to be the one who left. If I'd gotten you out sooner, maybe things would be different for us."

"Things are fine, Mom," he assured her, trying not to think back on the days he would come home from school to find his mother bruised and bloodied, or, worse, knocked out on the kitchen floor. "I don't know why I even asked. I guess I just needed to be sure you were okay."

At that, the worried frown spread across her aged face smoothed into a smile. "I'm just fine, honey. I have you."

An hour later Augustus bid his mother a good day then headed for what constituted the pathetic excuse for his company's office. They had a tiny shack on River Street where tourists could purchase tickets, and headquarters at his boss's entirely-too-large home downtown, but most meetings were held in a drafty storage unit that boasted a range of costumes and props guides used for their ghost tours and the special events the company held every Halloween.

It was cold, cramped, and sometimes smelled like feet, but their small group was used to it by now. Their boss wouldn't dare invite the riff-raff to his home office once a week. He considered himself far too important for that, and was far too cheap to spring for an actual office space.

How the rich stay rich, Augustus mused.

Augustus was the last to arrive. He nodded over to the other three guides—Voodoo, the tall and lanky man who always dressed in all black; Silas, with long blonde dreads that matched his equally pale skin; and Madame Mela, the early-twenties woman with a vibrant laugh and signature smirk—then turned to his boss. "Morning. Got your text for the meeting. So what's up?"

"Just waiting on you to arrive," Sonny Harvest replied pointedly. Sonny was a portly man, a former history professor turned ghost hunter turned businessman. Augustus liked to think of him as a fortunate buffoon, someone who had no real clue how the world worked yet somehow always managed to come out on top. It was the only explanation for the man's wealth, amazingly attractive young wife, and unexplainable positive outlook on life.

"I'm here now," Augustus replied as he took his place next to Mel. She's joined the team a few years ago, foregoing college in favor of life in sleepy Savannah and nighttimes talking about ghosts.

Mel shot him a playful grimace. "Fashionably late," she said out the side of her mouth.

"As always," he shot back at her with a grin.

Sonny clapped his hands twice to catch their attention. "Now that you're all here. I have had a wonderful idea!"

In the back, Voodoo groaned, knowing what such a proclamation meant. "As great an idea as Witch Week?"

Even before Sonny answered, Augustus prayed the idea would not be another Witch Week. Yes, that idea had been a great one in terms of turnout and profit, but if he never again had to spend an entire seven days helping little girls dress up like witches and take tours of the town while their parents enjoyed complimentary free drinks, it would be all too soon.

"Even better!" was Sonny's cheer, to the beat of another clap. "I've been doing some research and looking into numbers for our competitors. I even did a little secret shopping by calling and asking questions, pretending to be interested in a tour. And what I've discovered is that the other ghost tour companies are gaining on us. They are coming up with new and exciting things to draw in tourists."

Augustus and Mel shared a hesitant glance. Silas, always the calm and collected one, merely waited from where he was perched on a box.

"So we need to compete!" Sonny continued, hands waving animatedly. "Keep us relevant. People are coming in from all over now that Savannah is back on the map and we need to make sure *we* are their first stop."

"We already are," Augustus cut in. "We have a waiting list, for Christ's sake."

"*You* have a waiting list." His boss looked at him, then the other guides in turn. The comment sparked rolled eyes and bit-back sighs from the entire group. Augustus hated being singled out as the top guide, even if it was true, but he knew his boss wouldn't let it go. "You led Tessa Taylor on her tour, you knew Jason Waters before he saved the whole damn country. You have your own little fan club. I've seen that website someone made for your fans. I have my plans for everyone else with my wonderful new idea, but you, Augustus, well I have special plans for you."

He didn't like the sound of that claim, or the look of glee in Sonny's eyes. "What exactly does that mean?"

"It means we're going to start doing some daytime tours. Not the usual ghost and ghouls stories, but real history in the light of the sun to teach the public about our great city. But as we're doing this, we'll also throw in just enough intrigue to have them dying to come back at midnight." He laughed at his terrible joke, though no one else did.

"That's ridiculous," Voodoo spoke up from the back of the unit, where he had been pawing through a selection of old top hats. "People don't care about daytime history tours. That's what museums are for. They want to be spooked, and they want to be spooked at the witching hour."

"It wouldn't be exciting, anyway," Mel agreed, crossing her arms. "Savannah is cool and all, but during the day it's just like any other city."

Sonny crossed his arms as well, in a move they all knew was mocking rather than frustrated. "This isn't up for debate. We *will* be offering daytime tours, and everyone will have a schedule. But, Augustus, your will be our headliner. Posters, business cards, even a TV commercial. I've already set it all up. We are getting started this afternoon with the marketing materials, and, Augustus, I've already scheduled you a tour for tomorrow with a test group of tourists. We are going to make sure everyone knows that when they want to see Savannah, they better call us first!"

CHAPTER 6

After the others left, grumbling to themselves and leaving Augustus and Mel alone in the unit, Augustus turned to the woman he'd known for nearly ten years now. "What do you think about all this daytime tour shit?"

"You said it," she laughed, picking up a 1920s-style dress and holding it up to her slender frame. Occasionally she outfitted herself in older styles to suit her tours, finding the extra effort was appreciated by her tourists. "It's shit, but what are you gonna do."

"Be the face of daytime tours." Augustus grimaced, already dreading seeing himself in pamphlets and, god forbid, during a commercial break of some cheesy cable show. Sonny had made it clear that in one hour he was to report to a local media station to put together their "marketing package." But instead of voicing his concerns, and possibly pissing off his coworker, given their boss's clear favoritism, he found himself watching her as she admired herself in the mirror with the dress held out in front of her.

"It suits you," he told her, approving of the way the coral-colored lace accented her tanned skin and short blonde curls. The dress was a little long for her five-foot-three frame, but he knew women had a way of fixing things like that.

Peering at him through the mirror, Mel asked, "You think? I need to change up my act a little for one of my tours. I guess I've been lazy lately and haven't put much thought into getting into character. I was thinking this week I could dress up like one of the widows from our stories, or something."

"I like it." Augustus pushed himself off the wall and took a step closer. "You know, if you need some more ideas on ways to spice up your tours, I'd be happy to help. How about we discuss it over dinner?"

"You asking me out again?"

He caught her grin in the mirror and mimicked it. The offer had become a game to them, one he was determined to win. "Not asking. Cleverly persuading."

Mel carefully folded the dress and tucked it into her messenger bag. "You know I don't mix business with pleasure. Plus, you're old. You're like thirty-five." But she was laughing when she said it, even if it was true—he was ten years older than her.

"Breaking my heart," Augustus teased back. "You'll be eating those words when I'm a big star and all the ladies are begging for a tour from yours truly."

"Oh, please." Mel regarded him with a baleful stare as she set the bag over her shoulders. "We both know you'll still be begging me for a date."

With a chuckle, they closed up the unit and walked out together, going their separate ways at the main road.

*

Four hours later, Augustus learned an important lesson about himself—despite all his childhood dreams of being a famous actor worthy of winning an Oscar, he was not cut out for the silver screen. Whether it was the tacky script, the camera in his face, or the crowd of people watching and listening and expecting him to be perfect, acting was simply not in his future.

The photographs, though, those he excelled in. Augustus held his head high as he waltzed out of the studio. Sonny had, surprisingly, selected the perfect outfits and props for the magazine and poster shots, and the shoot had actually been fun.

"Augustus!" Sonny called out behind him. He jogged down the steps, huffing and puffing by the time he reached his guide. When he reached him, he held up a hand, signaling him to wait while he caught his breath, then held up a laminated poster. "Here's the mockup. What do you think?"

Damn, he works fast, Augustus thought as he looked over the poster, though he'd expect nothing less. When Sonny wanted something, he got it, and quickly. And, he had to admit, he did good work.

The top of the poster boasted the company's name in bold black letters, set against a slightly blurred Savannah landscape. Beneath the company name were the words *Now Offering Daytime History Tours!* along with contact and ticket information. And there, along the right side looking decidedly dashing and mysterious, was Augustus. His arms were crossed, body half turned as it faced the camera, lips turned up into a charming smirk. The clothing Sonny picked out were an intriguing mix of pirate, bootlegger, and old-time gangster, with loose sleeves, an open-collar white shirt with a black jacket, the collar popped to perfectly frame his jaw. His pants were black, while the pirate-style boots were worn and brown, with large buckles. And the sword at his waist, well that was the perfect accessory addition.

A strange combination, but damn did it work well for him. And though he wouldn't admit it out loud, he was looking forward to seeing what kind of fame these new advertisements earned him.

"Looks great," Augustus said honestly. "I'd sign up for a tour with this guy."

Sonny grinned and clapped a hand to the guide's back. "That's what we're going for! I'll be putting up dozens of these posters around Savannah, and I've hired a team to distribute smaller flyers to the surrounding cities. Our web guy is updating the website as we speak, and the commercial will start airing this weekend."

Augustus made a mental note to avoid all televisions that weekend as he replied, "Sounds good."

"Yes, it does. Now, don't forget, tomorrow is your first tour, eleven AM. You're meeting them at Monterey Square."

"I know. I looked over your itinerary. I'll be there." Offering his boss a wave, Augustus managed to escape further scrutiny of the poster and walked down the sidewalk. Now that work was done for the day, he had a sink to fix.

"Could use twenty bucks to buy the parts," he muttered. Payday wasn't until next week and he'd spent most of the last one on refilling his mother's medication.

A flutter of wings had Augustus pausing. He glanced around, then up, seeing the silhouette of a bird high in the oak tree above him. The sun shadowed its entire form, and, not knowing much about birds, he couldn't identify what kind it was, only noting that it seemed to be staring down at him.

"Weird." Shrugging it off, Augustus started to resume his walk, only to stop again when a cold breeze blew in suddenly, seeming to rustle only his hair and the shrub to his left. Warily, he looked down at the bush, brow furrowing as leaves floated away one by one on the wind, as though carefully uncovering....

"Well, shit," Augustus breathed when the wind stopped blowing and the leaves were gone, revealing a crumbled twenty-dollar bill. He retrieved the cash and stared down at it. The timing was certainly strange, him grumbling about wanting money only seconds before the unexpected wind that showed him hidden cash—and the exact amount he'd needed.

Brushing it off as coincidence, Augustus pocketed the money and continued his trek to the hardware store.

CHAPTER 7

The sun was high in a clear blue sky when his first daytime history tour began. Augustus met his group at Monterey Square and read off his roster, ensuring all ten people were there and ready for the two-hour walk through Savannah. Sonny had planned the route for the day, and while Augustus approved of it for the most part, he noted there was one stop left out, likely in hopes of securing an extra ghost tour later that night.

"Are we ready, visitors of Savannah?" he asked, purposely toning down his persona. Sonny had made it clear the daytime tours were to be serious and professional. Save the theatrics for midnight, he'd been instructed.

"First things first, I want to thank everyone for being a part of our pilot group for today's tour." *Even if you did get a free tour out of it*, he silently added. "If all goes well today, then we hope to offer many more in the future, taking groups all over Savannah. Today, we will see some of the city's most infamous homes, and stop for a traditional Southern-style lunch before we go our separate ways. Sound good?"

After everyone had nodded and smiled eagerly, Augustus said, "Perfect! Let's continue, to the corner of Abercorn and East Wayne!" With a dramatic wave of his arm, he all but flounced down the sidewalk, only rolling his eyes when his back was turned to the group. It felt so fake, right down to the toned-down pants and dress shirt he wore instead of his usual garb. He led them past a few side streets, listening to the quiet chatter behind him and hearing only interested comments that boosted his ego, and had him hoping the tour wouldn't be so boring after all.

They came to a stop at a beautiful multi-tier house with an expansive front balcony, winding staircase leading to the front door, and a back porch with wide white columns spanning two stories. In the daytime the home looked far less spooky, though the story he was about to tell would quickly remedy that.

"Here we are at Calhoun Square," he began, gesturing to the square of grass behind him. "Unbeknownst to many, this square was actually the location of a slave burial ground. As a result, there are many stories of people hosting pagan rituals, or witnessing paranormal activity. I mention this because of the home that sits right across the street, one famous for its own paranormal history."

Now he focused them on the residence. "This is known as the Espy House, once owned by a man named Carl Espy during the Prohibition. Carl was Savannah's own federal judge, but had a little side business to make some extra cash for his family. What was that side business?" He waited a beat to see if anyone would answer, then continued, "Carl was a bootlegger. That's right, a federal judge with a gig bootlegging alcohol."

A few expected chuckles and gasps followed the proclamation. "He never got caught?" a man in the back asked.

"He was a judge; Carl knew his way around the law." Augustus didn't actually know if Espy got caught—he'd never been interested enough to do the research, and hadn't had time to do any last night when he read about his route. "But his wife knew, and was brave enough to fight with him about it. I say 'brave enough' because it was well known just how bad a temper Carl had. Some even said he ruled his home with an iron fist. His-way-or-the-highway type of temper. It's said that in the midst of a terrible fight, Carl killed his wife."

Augustus held up a hand to emphasize his next point. "Now, there are some discrepancies with this story. Some accounts say it was his granddaughter who was killed; others say it was his wife. With so many conflicting sources, it's hard to know exactly who is right. Personally, I believe it was his wife, as more evidence points to this version being the truth. In any case, their daughter, who had been in the elevator at the time, witnessed the entire thing. But, because Carl was a federal judge, no charges were brought against him and he was never arrested."

Had this been a midnight tour, he would have added, *Some say the dead still haunts the house, wanting revenge but never able to get it, forever trapped within these walls*—with some added flair about recent hauntings. But he kept those words to himself. If these people wanted to know about spirits haunting the house, they'd have to sign up for a ghost tour.

Stepping to the side, Augustus allowed a few moments for the group to take pictures. Not so long ago, he would have laughed at how many of them peered down at their phone or camera screens, trying hard to find a ghost in a window or some sort of paranormal activity captured in film. Growing up, he'd never really believed in spirits, and even as a ghost tour guide saw the stories more as entertainment than fact.

Tessa Taylor and Jason Waters changed all that.

Before he could get lost in the memories, Augustus cleared his throat and caught the group's attention again. "Gruesome as it is, the story doesn't end with the wife's death. See, Carl Espy had a son, Wesley, who was a deacon at the Methodist church next door. Wesley apparently thought it would be a good idea to get involved with the girlfriend of a local gangster, who was affiliated with Carl, due to his bootlegging. Both Carl and the gangster told Wesley to end the affair, but his son didn't listen. Soon after, in 1934, Wesley went missing."

It surprised him that no one offered speculation as to what happened. His night crowds were usually livelier. "On December tenth, Wesley was found lashed to the house by the coal shoot, hanging upside down. At first glance it seemed he was dead, but when the boy who found him got closer, he realized Wesley was still alive, but barely. There was a lot of blood, and Wesley was making strange whimpering sounds. Upon closer inspection, the boy discovered that Wesley's...." A quick glance at the crowd reminded him there were a few children present, so Augustus chose his next words carefully.

"The boy discovered Wesley had been severely beaten, and that his genitals had been cut off and placed in his front coat pocket."

That got the reaction he was hoping for. Expressions of horror, awe, and just plain grossed out stared back at him. Before anyone could ask for more details, Augustus finished the story. "Carl tried to save his son by bringing in the top surgeon in the state, but Wesley passed away. The family covered up the truth about his death, saying he died from complications caused by a fall. It wasn't until years later that Wesley's sister, who also witnessed her mother's murder, finally spoke out and gave her version of the truth. No one believed her, of course, saying it was the ravings of a mad woman, but her version of what happened became legend, and the stories you here today."

Now, Wesley's spirit is said to haunt the balcony of his room, and that when you stand on or near the balcony you can hear footsteps as he paces back and forth. Again he added the words, years of habit preventing his brain from blocking them.

"What happened to the father? Carl Espy?"

Augustus offered the man who'd spoken up a quick glance and shrug, bored by the story now that it was over and he couldn't get into the haunted parts of it. "Well, some say he lived out the rest of his days miserable and alone." As a joke, he added, "Of course, that's hard to believe, considering all the gold he had buried in his basement."

He was about to laugh, when he saw a few of the guests exchange glances before looking back at him.

"For real?" one of them asked.

"Whose money was it? That gangster?" another questioned.

Holy shit, he thought, hiding a grin, *these idiots actually believe anything I tell them.*

It was time to test the waters, see just how far he could actually do with tourists who were eating up every word.

"Well, as I said earlier, Carl had ties with a local gangster. He was untouchable in life, given that he was a federal judge, but his death made him even more notorious in Savannah, especially considering the rumors around the circumstances of his wife and son's deaths."

He'd never really had to think up stories on the fly before, always telling the same twisted tales over and over again, night after night. A dramatic pause preceded, "It was only after his death police discovered Carl's true effect on the city. A close inspection of his house revealed a secret compartment in the floor of his kitchen, leading below the house into a tunnel he had carved out himself. And in that tunnel lay all the riches of the city that had gone missing over the past thirty years."

Wide eyes stared back at him, attention rapt on his words. Augustus bit back a chuckle. "Millions of dollars were squirreled away in trunks and suitcases and boxes. Bills, gold pieces, every kind of currency you could imagine. It was considered a large fortune, even back then."

"What did they do with the money?" someone asked from the front of the group, a young woman holding a digital camera up toward the house.

"Well, what do you do with a large fortune?" *Blow it, of course,* he said to himself, though to his tourists he replied, "Some of it was given back to the city, people and businesses they could provide it belonged to. Some went to parts of the city that had been unoccupied for more than a hundred years after the area had been ravaged by a devastating fire in 1820. The rest went to the community, helping to make the city a better place. Of course," he added with a wink, "it is widely believed that what officials found in the secret tunnel was just a diversion, that the real fortune was tucked away somewhere farther beneath or even behind the room, waiting to be discovered."

"You said the fire of 1820? Wasn't that the year Savannah was hit by the yellow fever outbreak?" the young woman asked again, ignoring the latter part of his tale.

Here we go. There was always someone in every group who asked about yellow fever, which ultimately led the conversation back to Jason Waters, which then led to Tessa Taylor. At least this woman's question was fluid and actually related to the conversation at hand.

"Yes," he replied, this time honestly.

"Do you think yellow fever will come back after last year's outbreak?"

"We have a cure," Augustus answered carefully, not wanting to give his true opinion, but the woman wasn't finished.

"But, Jason Waters came up with the cure, and he was Tessa Taylor's boss, and he only came up with the cure after she supposedly went into that house on Abercorn, so it all ties back, right?"

"And aren't we on Abercorn?" the man next to her asked. "Can we see that house next?"

"That house isn't part of this tour." And that was the reason why—Sonny knew these questions would come up, and wanted to sell the value of coming back at night. "If you want to hear more about Tessa Taylor, I recommend booking one of our nightly ghost tours. We get up close and personal with 432 Abercorn, and your guide will be happy to answer all your questions."

The woman stared at him, determined for answers but seeming to accept she wouldn't get any. "Do you believe what happened to her was paranormal, or just crazy?"

"I believe Tessa Taylor was haunted," he said, fighting the chill working its way up his spine. "But whether by her past or an evil spirit, no one will ever know."

CHAPTER 8

"How was your first day tour?" Gert asked her son almost as soon as he walked in the front door.

Hanging his jacket on the rack by the front door, Augustus looked over at his mother, who was sitting on the couch with a newspaper in hand. Doing the daily crossword, he figured, as she'd done every day for as long as he could remember.

"It was good," he answered, rounding the couch to take a seat next to her. A quick look at the paper showed he was right. The crossword was half filled out. "The crowd was excited and they seemed to appreciate the history lesson. Most of them wanted to know more about the ghosts and spirits side of things, so I let them know how to sign up. Time will tell if they actually do."

"I'm sure they will. Everyone loves your stories."

His mother smiled and it was contagious. He returned the gesture. Even if it did frustrate him at times to have to answer questions as soon as he came home, talking to her always made him feel better about himself. "Thirsty? I'm going to get something to drink."

"I'll come with you. I'd like a cup of tea."

Augustus helped her off the couch, staying by her side as they slowly walked the few steps into the kitchen. That was one benefit to living in a tiny house—his mother didn't have to go far for anything she needed. As he pulled a mug from the counter, he contemplated telling her what was truly vexing him, wanting to talk about it but worried how it would make him sound.

Couldn't hurt, he figured. If there was one person he could talk to without judgment, it was Gert. So he admitted, "Something weird did happen though."

"Oh? What?"

Thinking over the day, Augustus replied, "Well, I was doing the usual tour, giving history on a house and answering some questions. Then I thought I'd be funny and make a joke, but everyone believed the joke was true."

Gert smiled over at him. "Why is that strange, Nathaniel?"

He was close to being annoyed at the use of his real name, but decided to brush it off today. "Because usually there are people in the groups that have done *some* amount of research. Or they know BS when they hear it. But today everyone believed me, no questions asked. I guess it wasn't too outlandish a story, and since the whole point is to be a little spooked, but I would have thought they'd at least be hesitant to believe me."

"Well," Gert moved to the fridge, taking a half-gallon of milk out for her tea and a can of Coke for her son, "you are very charming in your tours. People believe you because they like you. You're very personable. It's why you're such a good tour guide."

He started to reply, but a splash of water on the counter next to him broke both of their attentions. Augustus glanced up to see a wet spot in the ceiling, the plaster starting to brown in a growing circular pattern. A few more splashes rained down, accompanied by small pieces of plaster. It was only then Augustus saw more water pooled behind the sink, a tiny river tracking across the counter and leading to the soggy wall.

"Oh, dear." Gert used the towel hanging from the fridge door to wipe the counter. Just watching his mother filled Augustus with anger, a growing rage tinged with regret.

"One of these days, Mom, I promise we'll have a nice place. This kind of stuff won't happen. I swear it."

Gert set down the rag and faced her son. "Nathaniel, I love our home. I don't care if it's old and I don't care if things break every now and then. That just means it has character."

"I care, Mom." Augustus picked up the towel and wiped up the water, wondering how he was going to pay to repair what he guessed was a leak in the roof when he'd just shelled out a few grand for a major plumbing issue a few months ago. "You deserve better than this. We *both* do."

"We make the best of what we can," was her reply, and he knew better than to respond. Gert didn't like to talk about the things they didn't have, often taking the blame herself because of who she chose to marry, and how long she chose to stay. "Now, how about we order some of that Chinese food you like so much?"

Augustus nodded. "Sounds good to me." He started to ask what she wanted, but hesitated when Gert froze, confusion crossing her aged face. "Mom? You okay?"

After too long a pause, Gert turned around and peered over at her son through glassy, narrowed eyes, frowning when she saw the towel in his hands. Her eyes followed his movements to the water on the counter, then up to the ceiling. "What happened to the roof? Is there a leak?"

Augustus bit back a sigh. Part of him wanted to ask if she was serious—they'd just been talking about the roof ten seconds ago. But the larger, more sensible part, knew she couldn't help it. "Don't worry about it, Mom. I'll take care of it. Promise."

Appeased, Gert kissed his cheek and slowly made her way to the living room, leaving Augustus to finish making her tea, then order the food and clean up the kitchen.

*

He went to bed early that night, planning to get up at dawn and start figuring out how the hell he was going to get his mother out of this shithole and into a nice place. He'd been putting off the home search for a long time, always worried about money, but he'd been saving up ever since business picked up.

In many ways, Tessa Taylor had been the best thing to ever happen to him. He got a raise and better tips during tours, his name was known throughout Savannah and beyond, and he'd even been approached to write a book about his experiences, which he was still considering. The local, and somewhat national, notoriety had been good for his bank account, but it wasn't yet good enough. So he had to keep milking it, first paying off all the debts he'd accumulated over the years, all the while trying not to think of all the ways Tessa Taylor had also been the worst thing to ever happen to him.

It started with the reporters, incessant insects looking for fresh blood at the first sign of a story. They'd camped out on his front lawn, visited him at work, hounded his mother when she tried to do a little gardening, signed up for tours in hopes of getting the scoop. Then came the cops, wanting to know the part he played in the Taylor Sibling Slaughters. And after the cops was Jason Waters.

Augustus still felt fear curdle in his gut when he thought of the man. Tessa hadn't been enough to make him believe the stories he told on a nightly basis. Even when she and her friend visited him after the tour, he couldn't decide if they were playing a joke, if the friend was just looking for a way to ask him out, or if they were two overzealous girls in need of something to do. Eventually, after she was admitted to—and later escaped from—the hospital, he'd chalked her up to having one too many screws loose, given her sordid past and abusive parents. But Jason...Jason he couldn't explain.

Jason Waters had made him a believer.

"Stop it," Augustus commanded himself. It was too easy to get lost in the memories, and he'd worked hard to force them out of his head. If he didn't think about it, he could pretend it never happened.

"At least you work again." He looked down at the leak-free sink he'd fixed last night. At least he could manage that much. Quickly he brushed his teeth and decided to forego a shower. He had another tour in the morning, so he'd get up early and look fresh for his second daytime venture through the city.

It seemed he'd only been in bed mere seconds before sleep overtook him. Dreamland took him to a place he recognized—the Denver, Colorado, neighborhood he'd lived in for most of his childhood, before his father left. Except it was different, not the same few streets filled with cheap modular homes so close together you could almost reach out and touch the house next door. Here, the houses were so run down they were nearly toppling over.

Wondering if he was dreaming or hallucinating, Augustus looked behind him, seeing nothing but an ocean of black, then faced forward and took a step out of the darkness, into his own personal hell. Somewhere up ahead he could hear children playing, music blasting, and even a gunshot in the distance. All the sounds he'd grown up with—including that of his father yelling from the trailer, four up from the neighborhood entrance.

"Fuck you," Augustus muttered beneath his breath, torn between staying rooted in place and racing to the trailer in hopes of saving his mother, or possibly his younger self, from whatever his father was shouting about. "All you ever did was make us feel like shit when you were the biggest sack of shit there ever was."

An unexpected and foreign fury welled within him, a need to destroy that voice and the man it belonged to. As though in tune with his emotions, the earth began to shift, quaking beneath his feet. Augustus dropped to his knees. He searched for something to hold on to or hide beneath, but quickly saw it would be no use. The entire neighborhood was crumbling—trees uprooting, car alarms blaring, homes shaking upon already-fragile foundations. Before he could comprehend what was happening, let alone how it was possible, it was over, a seconds-long destruction of the world he once knew.

"Oh, god."

The whisper escaped on a horrified breath when the ground finally stopped moving. Augustus rose on shaky legs, still feeling like he was rocking back and forth. The quake had lasted mere seconds, but judging by the scene in front of him, it might as well have lasted days.

Homes lay in ruin, cheap drywall and roofing and pieces of furniture sprawled across a dry and cracked earth. Water sprouted from busted pipes, flooding what little grass managed to grow here. Cars were toppled over, some with interior contents spilling out over torn-up sidewalks, others crushed beneath thick oak trees uprooted at the base and laying sideways across the narrow streets. Telephone poles were split right up the middle, wires sparking as they swung from branches and rooftops.

But that wasn't what had Augustus's breath catching in his chest. He could handle the sight of trees and homes and cars ripped apart. What made him want to vomit was the blood. So much of it seeping down the pavement, splattered across white walls like masterpieces painted by death himself. So much blood he had to wonder how it was possible that one quake could produce such a disaster.

And, making the scene even worse, mixed with the blood were the whimpers. People were injured—children were injured. That fact had Augustus forcing himself through the wreckage in search of anyone he could help.

The first body he came upon was that of a young woman leaning against a car with its tires popped. He recognized her as an old neighbor, a nice enough woman with an unfortunate heroin addiction. Brown eyes were wide in panic, but also lifeless. His own gaze traveled the length of her body to find a piece of metal sticking out of her stomach. A gag worked its way up his throat and he had to turn away.

A few more steps had him tripping over a foot extended out from beneath a slab of wall. A child's bare foot, the knee it connected to squished into fragments. Not able to handle the thought of what lay beneath the wall, Augustus forced himself to look away. He couldn't do this. He couldn't help people if the very sight of their pain made him pass out.

But he had to know. He couldn't leave, not until he checked one house, and one person.

His feet led him to his old home. The trailer was almost flattened, which didn't bother him. He'd always hated this place. But, he also knew what lay inside, and so he removed the debris piece by piece, effectively digging out the kitchen, sweating beneath the burning sun until he finally saw flesh.

A hand, decorated with a scarred gold band and a spider web tattoo above the thumb. His father's hand. More digging produced an arm, and it was with a sickening gasp Augustus realized the arm was severed at the shoulder, bone and tendon bleeding across the earth. A need to see the rest had him shoving aside the rest of the rubble, the skin on his fingers tearing against the broken concrete and wood, until he could see his father's face. His pale and lifeless face bashed in by a fallen light fixture or window, if the glass embedded into his formerly brown eyes were any indication.

"Can't say I feel sorry for you," Augustus spoke down to his father, wishing he were real and not just a mirage in his dream. One hand reached out to check for a pulse, his fingers touching cold skin and coming away wet with sticky blood.

"For you, brave soul who has seen so much darkness and lived to speak of it," a smooth voice spoke behind Augustus. "I layeth the city at your feet."

Augustus spun, momentarily forgetting his father's body behind him as he took in the sight of the sudden stranger. A gasp escaped before he could stop it. This...thing, this creature, standing before him was something he couldn't have imagined even in his nightmares.

Its body resembled a crow, shiny black feathers reflecting off the afternoon sun. But its legs were those of a man, the skin rough and weathered, ending in feet clad in hard black boots. Human-like arms, too, sprouted from feathery shoulders, while large black wings were spread in a grand display. Worst of all, though, was the creature's face. Half man, half crow, with beady eyes and a beak where a mouth should be.

It took a moment for Augustus to find his voice. "What... Who are you?"

"I am the servant to your greatest desire," the beast replied with a foreign tongue. "I am the one they call Raum, and I do this all in your honor." One arm swept in a gesture to the crumbled city around them.

"You...you did this for me?" Another glance around had his stomach roiling. The blood, the bodies, the destruction. While it gave him some amount of sick satisfaction to see his father's broken body at his feet, the rest of it made him sick. "I never asked for this."

"You didn't have to," the creature called Raum replied. "I know what desires lie in your heart."

Bolstered by a dream-state courage, Augustus replied, "Clearly not. I have no desire to see people killed and entire neighborhoods in pieces. Especially kids being hurt."

"You desire the death of the one who hurt you most."

"No," he argued, surprising even himself. "Do I feel sorry for him, laying there bashed to pieces? Not even a little bit. But I don't sit around thinking of different ways he could die. To be honest, I hardly ever think of him at all."

"You need not think his name to wish his death. His destruction is the greatest revenge."

"No," he said again, finally giving voice to the truth he'd discovered after years of letting his heart fill with hate. "Living, accomplishing all the things he said I could never do, actually becoming someone important, is the best revenge."

To his relief, the beast didn't seem angry, only disappointed. His head bowed in acceptance. "I see," he replied in a formal and dismissive tone. "Your heart calls for the one who brings you fortune. The one who will serve your greatest lies."

Augustus frowned. "What lies?"

But the creature was gone with a flap of wing, the harsh, cold air blasting Augustus awake.

CHAPTER 9

The time on his phone read 10:02. For a moment Augustus could only stare, knowing he'd fallen asleep around 10 PM on the dot and wondering how it was possible only a couple minutes had passed when his dream seemed to last so long.

His body felt wired, like he'd just spent the last hour wading through rubble and witnessing the death of so many innocent people. Sleep would be impossible now. With a sigh, Augustus rose and headed to the kitchen, hoping a beer or two would kick his body back into unconsciousness. A *dreamless* unconsciousness. His mother had already gone to bed, leaving the house dark as he quietly made his way through.

In the kitchen, he navigated using the nightlight he'd put in for his mother, blinking in the bright light of the fridge. He reached in to pull out a beer, then froze when he saw the smear of red on the back of his hand and spreading down to his palm. He stared at his hand, his fingers, at the blood coating his flesh, then his body caught up with his brain and he stumbled back, hitting the edge of the counter.

Augustus grabbed a towel and began wiping at his hand. Strange sounds of panic escaped his lips as he scrubbed, then rushed to the sink and all but flung the water on and shoved his hands beneath the stream. But the blood wouldn't come off. It stained his skin, clinging to every pore no matter how hard he wiped.

"Come off. Come off," he mumbled, his voice laced with fear as he grabbed the sponge and scrubbed as hard as he could using the abrasive side.

"Nathaniel?"

Startled, Augustus spun around, forgetting about the running water as he shoved his bloody hand behind his back. "Mom," he said breathlessly, trying hard to hide the panic and knowing he failed miserably.

"Are you okay? What's wrong with your hand? Why are you scrubbing at it like that?"

"Nothing."

Gert shot him an unamused frown and approached, reaching for his arm. Knowing better than to argue, he let her pull his hand from behind his back, his mind working for an excuse.

I cut myself shaving.

Slipped on the way to bed.

Had a dream Dad died and when I woke up my hand was covered in his blood.

"Are you being smart with me?" Gert asked, and Augustus looked down to see his hand was perfectly fine—no blood, no evidence of his dream-turned-reality.

"What?" Pulling his hand back, Augustus turned it over, holding his arm up in front of his face, not sure how to accept the fact that not a speck of blood was to be found on his skin. It was just his hand, same as always. "Um…I guess I was just seeing things. Too tired, you know?"

Gert's expression turned sympathetic. "My son, working so hard. You go and get some sleep and don't worry about a thing. It will all look better in the morning."

He wasn't so sure about that, but followed her orders, bringing three beers he planned on downing as quickly as possible. Maybe if he didn't have to think about the disappearing blood act, he could pretend it never really happened at all.

*

Gert's sympathy extended to the Will O'Wisp as it watched Augustus return to his bedroom. It could feel the man's confusion and denial, such familiar emotions for the poor souls who found themselves lost to the bid.

Augustus Jones was a different story though. He knew bad things happened to people who entered the house, even if he couldn't put a name to those things. And yet he willingly entered anyway. It was for a noble cause, but the man would suffer the consequences anyway…as would the child.

The Will O'Wisp could see them both as they suffered the same bewilderment and fear. But it worried most for Augustus. The man was tormented in so many ways, haunted by memories long before spirits, and the descent into madness would be far more devastating.

A flash of light tugged the Will O'Wisp from its observation. It looked down at the single remaining flame demanding to make its presence known. But there would be no solace for either one of them tonight, just as there would be none for Augustus Jones.

There was only death at the hands of a demon finally freed from its prison.

CHAPTER 10

"Augustus! My star!"

Sonny clapped Augustus on the back when he approached the River Street kiosk, ready to check in and get his schedule for the next few days and nights. Standing just outside the booth and leaning against the counter, Mel mocked Sonny behind his back with an exaggerated grin.

"What's up, Sonny?"

"I'll tell you what's up!" His boss shoved a piece of paper at Augustus. "We've more than doubled our ghost tour signups since we started offering the daytime tours—and we just started three days ago! More than half the guests who attended your first two day tours came back and immediately signed up for a ghost tour. And the tour Voodoo led yesterday had a twenty percent signup! I knew this was a good idea."

"Happy for you, boss," Augustus answered dryly, not interested at all in how many people signed up. As long as he got paid, and got his tips, he was happy. "Just here for the schedule."

Not to be deterred, Sonny asked, "Did you see the commercial?"

"Nope."

"I did," Silas piped up as he approached, taking his schedule from Sonny. He shot Augustus his usual lazy grin and offered a bow. "We're in the presence of ghost tour royalty, ladies and gentlemen. Now, let us embark on a grand adventure!"

"Where all Savannah's memories are waiting to be discovered!" Mel continued, repeating the lines from the commercial. She and Silas laughed, while their boss merely shook his head.

"Mock my commercial all you want, but it's bringing in business. Which may result in a raise for the people who show support." As he'd known it would, the comment sobered the two right up and they looked at him hopefully. "Give it a few months, my fearless guides. Don't I always come through for you?"

None could deny that, so they didn't reply. Sonny nodded at their silence. "Just as I suspected. Now, off with you! Can't have you three clogging up my kiosk when there are tourists looking to buy tickets!" He scurried behind the counter to prepare for opening. "Augustus, I look forward to hearing from your tourists after tonight. Madame Mela, you keep dressing up in those costumes and getting those great reviews and we might have to think about a whole new avenue for your tours! Silas…air out before our next tour. You smell like marijuana."

Mel snorted, then stuck her tongue out at Silas when he shot her the finger. But he walked away with a grin, not at all ashamed or embarrassed, while Sonny called after him with another shower recommendation.

Rolling his eyes at his boss's back, Augustus tucked the schedule into his pocket, then turned his attention to the beautiful blonde still leaning against the counter watching the crowd pass by. "River Street's in full swing today."

Mel's head slowly turned as she glanced at him before focusing on the crowd. "Worst pickup line ever."

Sidling up next to her, Augustus pretended not to hear her. "You, me, and two giant cheeseburgers and a shared plate of fries," he invited with a mischievous grin. "I'll even let you pick the place."

"Tempting, but you know the drill, Augustus," Mel replied, one eyebrow playfully cocked. "Business and pleasure, remember?"

Determined not to let her get away this time, Augustus propped a hand up on the counter behind her and attempted his best charming grin. When he spoke next, it was with a slightly raspy tone that made him sound like he had a cold, but he went with it, hoping it made him sound seductive. "Aw, come on, babe. I seem to remember you saying you couldn't wait to go out with me."

He expected the joke to be met with a huff or a mocking slug to the shoulder, and was surprised when Mel's head cocked to the side, her expression thoughtful. "I did?" Then her face changed, a smile creeping over her face. "You're right. I did say that last time, didn't I? Well, then I guess we better go get those cheeseburgers. Let's go to Zoe's. They have the *best* chocolate milkshakes."

Dumbfounded, and a little suspicious she was just messing with him, Augustus wordlessly helped her into her coat when she grabbed it from the counter, racking his brain to try to remember any time Mel had actually said those words. Except he knew, deep down, all she'd ever done was turn him down.

So why was she taking his statement at face value, when they both knew he was lying? And what "last time" was she talking about? The last time he asked her out, she told him he was too old for her.

It reminded him of the other day, when the tourists automatically believed his claim about Carl Espy and the stolen gold. No one even questioned him or said he was full of shit. Maybe she was just getting him back for all his flirting.

Let's see if she goes for this. Bet she'll drop the act after this one.

"I also remember you saying you'd even treat me to dinner. You know, to make up for all those dates you turned down."

Mel laughed and nodded. "Sounds fair to me."

Her back turned, she didn't see the way Augustus's mouth dropped or the falter in his step. He recovered quickly—on the outside, anyway—and joined her on the sidewalk. They made the five-minute walk down to Zoe's in near silence, Augustus reflecting on what the hell was happening and Mel seeming to be lost in her own world as well.

He waited until they were led to a booth and had their drink orders taken before saying, "I'm glad we could finally do this," and keeping his eyes trained on her, searching for any sign she was just trying to make a fool out of him.

"Me too," she replied, not needing to look at the menu. Instead she grinned over at him, her smile full of happiness and innocence. Too much innocence, he noted. Mel was a good actress for her tours, but not *that* good.

"So…what made you finally give me a chance?"

She thought about it for a moment, slender fingers toying with a napkin. "I don't know. I guess I figured, what could it hurt? Remember the other day when you asked me out? The day Sonny first told us about the daytime history tours? I guess I thought about what you said, about how I'd regret not going out with you when I had the chance, because someone else was interested in being with you, and if you said yes then it would be too late. And I realized, I didn't want to risk that happening, and regret it. So, here we sit. I'm giving you that chance."

Again she smiled, her entire face lighting up. Augustus returned a small grin of his own, while his mind struggled to understand what the hell she just said. Yes, he remembered that day in the storage unit, but he also remembered it differently.

Yes, he'd told her she would regret it, but only when he became a big star and all the ladies wanted tours from him. He never said anything about there being someone else, let alone some other woman he actually had lined up and ready for a date. Either she was remembering that day differently, or he was.

Or maybe something else entirely was happening, something dark and unnatural, and all the weird events happening lately were leading up to the big revelation.

The waitress brought their drinks, two large chocolate milkshakes, and took their food order. Once she was out of view, Augustus finally replied, "Well, I'm glad you said yes. I know you think I'm just some old creepy guy, but, for what it's worth, I really do like you."

"I like you too. And I don't think you're some old creepy guy. You're not even old."

Now he knew he was dealing with either an extremely talented liar, or an unexplainable force of nature making the girl of his dreams act like she suddenly came down with a case of selective amnesia. Her confusion made him feel like he was losing his own mind.

He needed answers, and she was the best person to get them from.

"So, *Madame Mela*, you're into the whole voodoo and mystic shit this town subscribes to, right?"

Mel huffed and took a sip of her shake. "Well when you put it that way, it sounds so exciting."

"You know what I mean. You really enjoy looking into all the stories about rituals and people going crazy after trying to conjure up spirits, things like that. I guess I was just curious...."

"If it's real?" she finished for him. When he nodded, she shrugged and looked out the window. River Street was bustling with activity, the shops open, boats slicing through water. It was a light, happy day. "Personally, I think so. There are dark forces out there, and whether people want to believe in them or not, they will find you, if you are the one they want."

He didn't like the sound of that. "What would make a person someone they want?"

"Could be any number of things. Sometimes the person has something the spirit wants. Money, power, a body easy to take over. Sometimes it's just bad luck, a person being in the wrong place at the wrong time."

Like breaking into a haunted house to find a stupid teenage kid. "What happens if you find those dark forces?"

Mel frowned and leaned back in the booth. "Well, you know the stories about the rituals occult members used to perform in the cemetery. There are hundreds of stories that tell the horrors and give warnings about messing with dark forces."

"I remember," Augustus reflected, thinking back to his early research on the city of Savannah. "Perform a ritual before midnight, you're in the clear. Perform a ritual after midnight, and you risk opening the portal to Hell."

"In a matter of speaking. The rituals aren't always satanic. Sometimes people want to speak to loved ones who died. Others, well, they think they are being dangerous and living on the edge, and perform an absolutely pointless ritual that does nothing except give them the creeps."

"But sometimes it's real."

"Sometimes," she confirmed. "But why do you care anyway? You don't believe a single word of it." Mel paused when their food arrived, taking a moment to slather her fries in ketchup and take another few sips of her shake before asking, "What brings this up, anyway? Finally getting into the spirit of Savannah after all these years? Thinking of breaking into the cemetery and performing a ritual?"

Not at the moment, he replied silently. Some small part of his brain was wondering if he'd need one in the near future. That, or a bed in the nearest mental ward. "Nah," he said instead. "Just trying to come up with some better stories for the day tours."

Mel eyed him curiously, but her reply was cut off by the shrill ring of Augustus's cell phone. He glanced at the screen, not recognizing the number and answering anyway. Starting to tease him about taking calls at the table, Mel made to take the phone away, stopped by the look of alarm in his eyes.

"What's wrong?" she asked, but her words went unheard. Augustus was already on his feet, racing out of the restaurant.

CHAPTER 11

"What were you thinking, Mom?"

He'd arrived at the hospital only twenty minutes ago, all but forcing his way through the ER. A doctor had given him a quick rundown before allowing him in to see his mother. Now he was staring down at her with a mix of relief, anger, and flat-out confusion.

Gert looked up at him from the bed, the tubes in her nose more for precaution than necessity. The right side of her face was bruised and her cheek bandaged, her right arm was in a sling, and, though he couldn't see her left leg, he knew the ankle was in a cast. "I'm fine, Nathaniel."

"Fine? Look at you, Mom. You are not *fine*." The word came out more forcefully than he'd intended. Augustus took in a deep breath to calm his nerves, then tried again. "Mom. I told you I would take care of the ceiling. Why on earth did you try to fix it yourself? How did you even get the ladder in the house?"

"I'm old, not an invalid," Gert snapped back, but he could see the puzzlement mixing in her blue eyes and suddenly he knew why she'd tried to fix the leak. She didn't remember the conversation in the kitchen the night before, and wasn't in her right mind when she decided to go at it alone. The moment he'd feared—having to make the decision for her mental health—was rapidly approaching, though he wouldn't make the call today. He couldn't, not with her so bandaged and bruised in an uncomfortable hospital bed.

Feeling himself calm down, Augustus sat on the edge of the bed. "You're right. I'm sorry I yelled. I was just worried about you."

A smile replaced the scowl on Gert's black-and-blue face. "There's my charming son. Maybe he could sneak me in some chocolate?"

"I think he can manage that," Augustus laughed. "How about I get you your favorite book, the paper so you can do the crossword, and a big box of chocolate?"

"That sounds lovely, Nathaniel."

"Good." She would have to stay the night due to hitting her head, so he would bring her all of that, along with fresh clothes, that afternoon, after speaking with the doctor about next steps for her health. "In the meantime, I'll see about getting that roof fixed. No more ladders, okay?"

He waited until she smiled and nodded, then added, "Get some rest, Mom. I'll be back soon."

*

He headed home immediately, his cell phone never leaving his hand the entire way. Every contractor he knew was already plugged into his contacts—he'd needed them a lot lately—and one of them had agreed to meet at his house for a quick look.

Now Augustus stood in the kitchen with Marcus Heinz, one of the few contractors who hadn't quoted him a small fortune with every repair needed. "So, what's the damage?"

Head up near the ceiling, Marcus took a long moment to continue his observations before answering, one hand pushing against the damp plaster. "I'll have to get up in the attic to be sure, but this amount of water and the dampness I can already see and feel, my guess is that it's a pretty significant roof leak that's being going on for quite some time, so it's going to be more than just patching up the ceiling here."

"Okay, so give me a low and a high."

"Low, couple hundred, maybe? Depends on the repair work needed on the other side, and you'll need a little work behind the sink down there where the water damaged the drywall. You could leave it since it's not too big a deal just yet, but you run the risk of mold. High, not sure yet. I'm guessing a few thousand, at least, if it's a prolonged leak we're dealing with."

Augustus groaned inwardly. A few thousand, just what he needed. "Okay…well, you know where everything is if you want to go up and take a look. Any way we can get this done by the end of the week? I'd rather have this done by the time Mom comes home from the hospital. The doctor wants to keep her for a few days."

Climbing back down the ladder, Marcus pulled out his phone. Augustus assumed he was looking at his calendar. "Yeah, I think I can swing it if we can get the materials within the next couple days. I have some of it on hand so I can get the guys in tonight to start tearing out the damaged areas. I'll need payment right when the job is done though, in cash. I won't be able to wait like we did last time. I'll also need half upfront for materials. Just give me a minute to do a little more looking around, then I'll come up with the quote."

"That's fine," Augustus sighed. His luck of "repair now, pay later" was finally up, it seemed. "I'm going to go crunch some numbers. Let me know when you're ready with a quote."

CHAPTER 12

Five thousand dollars. He was going to owe Marcus five grand by the end of the week, and that was only to cover the immediate repair needed. He'd need another four thousand to fix all the damage caused by a leak that had apparently been polluting his entire attic for many months, leading to an unbelievable amount of wood rot and mold.

He couldn't have his mother living in such squalor. Not only was it embarrassing, but her health couldn't take it anymore. At the very least, Augustus planned to start searching for a cheap—and temporary—apartment, but in the meantime he'd have to fix the roof and attic if he ever wanted to sell the house. The only money he had was in savings, savings he'd been squirreling away for the past few years in hopes of getting his mother into a decent home.

So now he sat in front of a giant, glossy-top oak desk, waiting while the banker on the other side took a glance through his finances. He'd known Shelby Cross for a while, having spoken to her more than once about what he'd need to do for a home loan, and he hoped she could help him out now.

"I know it's not as much as last time I was in here," he said nervously as she looked through his account information. "I had to take some out for a plumbing issue a little while ago. I've been trying to build my savings back up since then, but with Mom's health and the house and everything, it's been hard."

Shelby didn't immediately reply, so he continued, unable to stop his rambling, "I was hoping I could look into a loan. The house needs a lot of work before I can put it on the market, but I think with a small loan I can get enough done to pass inspections. So I guess I also want to see what you think my chances are for a home loan. I haven't checked my credit score in a while, but I'm not late on any payments."

When he paused to take a breath, his banker and financial consultant said, "We can discuss all of that. But first we need to figure out your savings. You're going to need a lot more than this to buy a home. Even if we were able to get you into a first-time buyer program and negotiate on closing costs, you're still going to need a substantial amount to cover all other initial costs of buying. Inspections, appraisal fees, things like that."

"Right." He tried to sound self-assured and knowledgeable. "So let's talk. What are my options?"

The frown she directed at the computer had him swallowing back a sigh. "Well…I think we can work with this in regards to a small loan for your home repairs. Otherwise I would recommend doubling your savings, at the very least. Even if we get you into a program with the lowest possible rates and you have to pay all or some closing costs on, say, a house that costs one-forty, you're still looking at anywhere from five to eight thousand. And that's not counting those extra expenses I mentioned."

"That just doesn't sound right," Augustus sighed, running a hand through his hair. "I should have all that and more." He'd been saving for so long, yet it felt like he was seeing so little reward. Too many house and health issues, not enough payout, and possibly simply having no idea how to actually budget properly.

Shelby pressed her lips together and glanced over at the computer. Her nails clicked across the keyboard. "Higher?"

Not hearing the confusion in her voice, Augustus replied, "Yeah. With how much I've been saving, it should be double that amount. Sixteen thousand at least. I don't understand how this is happening."

"I don't either." At her perplexed tone, Augustus glanced over at her, surprised to see her looking so distressed. "We've never made this kind of mistake before."

Now just as confused as Shelby, Augustus sat back, trying to decipher her meaning. "Um...what?"

"What was the amount the last time you looked?" Shelby continued as though she hadn't heard him. "You said double at least, which would actually put you at around...seventeen thousand, three hundred, not sixteen." Her eyes turned to meet his, narrowing at the way he stared at her. "Is that incorrect?"

More.

The voice appeared in his head without caution or invitation. It was a raspy, cold sound, almost gleeful in its greed. And it scared the shit out of Augustus.

You deserve more. Take what you deserve.

There was no one else in the office except the two of them. Shelby didn't appear to hear anything out of the ordinary. Yet Augustus was certain he'd heard a voice not once, but twice, and it certainly wasn't one he'd ever heard before.

"Mr. Jones?"

Augustus blinked, realizing he'd been sitting there staring into space while Shelby continued to ask him questions. "Sorry, I was... thinking about finances."

"Right. About your finances. As I said, we've never made such a large mistake before, but if you are certain you had more money in your account, I'm sure there is something we could do. I'd just need to see statements to show the flow of money. Deposits, transactions, and so on."

Entirely baffled by her line of questioning, Augustus took a moment to think. She believed one random and frustrated comment that he should have more money. He hadn't even been trying to get more out of her; he'd just been stressed out and venting, and she'd taken it as fact. Just like Mel had taken him at his word that she wanted to go on a date with him.

Discover the power of your voice, the mysterious intruder came again. *Say what you want, what you deserve.*

Like a vision appearing in dream, Augustus saw the words he should speak. As he read them in his mind, he got a strange feeling in his chest knowing he would be believed. It was a feeling of power, and he liked it.

"I...I don't have any statements," he tested, his voice coming out rougher than usual. He cleared his throat before adding, "Never needed them before. I just know there was double the amount in my savings account." He felt dirty speaking the lie, and, yet, oddly authoritative. For all he knew, Shelby might throw him out of the bank, or even call the cops on him. The possibility of getting caught only added to the feeling of power.

The expression on the young banker's face showed a mix of hesitation and uncertainty before finally settling on resigned. "I understand, Mr. Jones. I apologize for such a terrible mistake. We can definitely get this resolved within the next few days. In the meantime, let me give you something for your troubles."

"Not necessary." He held up a hand, just wanting to get the hell out of there. "I, uh, have another appointment."

"I insist." Shelby followed him to the door, gesturing for him to wait while she went to another room and unlocked it, disappearing inside for a few seconds. When she reemerged, she handed him an envelope. "Please forgive us for such an error, Mr. Jones. I will let you know when the matter is resolved."

*

Only after the bank had disappeared behind him did Augustus take a look inside the envelope, blowing out a breath when he saw the five hundred-dollar gift card. Even if he got nothing from his trip to the bank, he sure as hell was going to get something out of this.

"Grocery store, gas, Mom's medicine, and a new pair of boots it is. Really living large, Jones," he laughed to himself, annoyed by his practical purchases but knowing they were for the best.

He'd parked a street over from the bank, his car tucked beneath a sprawling oak within walking distance of the Colonial Park Cemetery. He walked quickly, afraid someone from the bank would come running after him and accuse him of fraud…or whatever the hell that was. As he approached his vehicle, a fluttering sound had him pausing, turning around slowly.

A stork stood in the middle of the road. It stared at him through beady black eyes, in contrast to the stark white of its feathers. Augustus wasn't much of an animal person and had no idea what kind of stork it was, or why it was just standing there looking at him, but something about it creeped him out and reminded him of the bird from the other day.

Maybe he had a shadow, he considered with a roll of his eyes. Some demented bird looking for a handout in the form of bread, or whatever storks ate. He turned away, reaching for the car door handle, blinking when something red glinted in his eye.

Glancing down, Augustus saw a stone the size of his thumbnail sitting in the grass next to his car. He leaned down to retrieve it, rubbing dirt off the stone with his finger. It was a ruby, he realized, and a beautiful one at that. Likely worth a good sum of cash. But what the hell was a ruby doing in the grass, on the side of a Savannah road?

Augustus glanced over his shoulder, but the stork was gone. A quick perusal of his surroundings showed he was alone on the street, so he pocketed the stone and got in the car, heading home. He'd figure out the authenticity of the stone later. Right now, he had a contractor to deal with.

CHAPTER 13

Three days later, Augustus sat in the hospital parking lot, staring down at his phone in shock. He had to pay Marcus today after visiting his mother and decided to check his account, only to find Shelby had been serious about correcting a mistake that was never really a mistake in the first place.

His savings account currently read just over seventeen thousand dollars. He'd never seen that high a number in his account in his entire life. And now it was just sitting in there, completely undeserved, obtained through a lie the banker never should have believed.

"What the fuck is happening?" he asked no one in particular, and then directed a question to himself. *Should I keep it or give it back?*

It was dishonest, flat-out wrong.

He needed the money, not for himself, but for his mother.

It was essentially stealing.

From who? The bank had enough money; they could spare a little extra.

He wasn't a criminal, someone who lied to get their way, for profit.

If he gave it back, he'd never be able to help his mom and get them both out of the house.

Such doubt, said the harsh voice that ordered him to lie about the money in the first place. *Do you not deserve a little luxury in your life?*

He did, Augustus realized. He worked damn hard every day, came home exhausted yet still took care of someone else and an entire household. So what if he took a little extra cash as payment for a whole lifetime of hard work?

So he logged out of his account and shoved his phone in his pocket, deciding that if the bank wanted to call it their mistake, then he wasn't going to stop them. This time, anyway. If it happened again he would say something.

At least, he thought he would.

Pushing all thoughts of money from his mind, Augustus entered the hospital and headed straight to his mother's room. When he walked in, she was speaking with a nurse, likely trying to get ice cream or chocolate brought to her room.

"Nathaniel!" she said happily as he entered, then touched the nurse's arm. "This is my son, Nathaniel. The one I told you all about. He is the sweetest young man you'll ever meet."

The nurse, a young and pretty woman with close-cropped black hair and lively green eyes, smiled over at him. "Pleased to meet you, Nathaniel."

"Augustus," he corrected her, instantly realizing it wasn't chocolate his mother wanted from the nurse, but a potential daughter-in-law. And he wasn't even a little bit interested. Bypassing the nurse, he went to his mother's bedside and handed her a pair of her favorite pink, fuzzy socks. "Finally found them buried in the back of your closet. Want me to put them on?"

"Don't be silly. I can put on my own socks," Gert insisted, though as soon as she moved she winced in pain, her bruised ribs protesting. Not wanting to embarrass her, Augustus simply shifted to the end of the bed and carefully placed the socks on her feet, the left one awkwardly stretching over the cast.

"Thank you," Gert relented with a small smile. She reached out for her son's hand, then asked, "When can I go home? I don't like it here. It's very noisy and I can't watch my shows in peace."

"A couple more days," the nurse answered for Augustus. She patted Gert's shoulder. "Just need to make sure your body is healing and the swelling on your head goes down. But you're looking better and better, so just hang tight a little while longer."

With that, she bid them both good-bye, claiming to be back later around lunchtime. "Lunch," Gert scoffed. "They have very poor excuses for food around here."

The bitterness in her tone worried Augustus. His mother had never been the type to make disparaging remarks, and he hoped it was just because she was tired and homesick. "I'll bring you something good for dinner tonight," he promised. "I have a tour at noon and another at eleven tonight, and I'm meeting the contractor this afternoon, so I'll be by after I speak with him."

"Fine." Gert sighed, then her eyes widened and she pointed behind him, at the window. "Would you look at that! What a beautiful stork, just sitting on that branch watching us."

Swallowing hard as his body threatened to freeze, Augustus slowly turned. Sure enough, a stork was perched on one of the trees just outside the room, standing perfectly still and watching them intently. It never moved, statue-like, except for the occasional blink and ruffle of feathers in the wind. Though he guessed all birds of the same species looked more or less the same, he swore this was the bird who had visited him twice before.

So what the hell did it want now?

Not searching for the answer, Augustus stalked to the window and grabbed hold of the curtains, thrusting them closed. Then he looked back at his mother. "Let's make a list for dinner. Whatever you want, I'll make sure you have it."

They created a meal together, Augustus mentally planning to stop by the store and use what was left of that gift card to purchase some special treats for Gert. When they were done, he rose from the chair next to the bed and kissed her forehead. "I'll be back soon, promise. Just need to get these couple things taken care of."

Gert nodded and settled back against the pillows he fluffed

for her. "Such a good boy," she said, then closed her eyes to let sleep take her.

*

He hated to admit it, but Sonny was right. His daytime tours *were* a wonderful idea. Augustus had led a group of fifteen around Savannah, leaving out all the juicy parts about ghosts and demon possessions, and still ended up with double the tips he'd earned from his last ghost tour.

The money was burning a hole in his pocket when he returned home to check on the repairs. All he wanted to do was give Mel a call and see about a second date to make up for running out on her before. Sure, she'd understood, and even visited his mother once when he was working, but he needed to make it up to her, especially now that she'd finally caved on dating him.

Caved, or was magically convinced. He still wasn't sure which.

Finding the contractor in the kitchen, Augustus asked, "How's it looking?"

Marcus wiped his hands on a rag hanging at his waist. His hair was disheveled and face smudged with grime, but his expression was otherwise pleasant. "Pretty good. Got the leak patched up and the rotted support beams in that area replaced. If you are planning on selling the place, an inspector will probably point out that area, just as a head's up, but I can guarantee no rot is left in those beams. I also patched up the ceiling where the water came through."

"Great." Augustus glanced up at the ceiling, impressed. The contractor worked quickly, and worked well, which was what he needed most.

"There are the other areas we discussed before that will need to be addressed as soon as possible, but for now, you're out of any immediate trouble, except for the mold. So I'd get that taken care of ASAP." He walked over to the sink and pointed to the backsplash. "Got this cleaned up too. There was some rot behind the sink, so we replaced the wall and painted it, and sealed the area around the counter. You won't be seeing any leaks in there any time soon."

Which was all Augustus cared about at this point. "Looks nice. Thanks for getting this all done so fast."

"No problem." Marcus started loading tools into a bag on the floor. "So I just need the remaining four thousand cash, and I'll be out of your hair."

Augustus paused, eyeing the contractor suspiciously. "Four thousand? I already gave you half of the quote for materials and the deposit. I should only owe you another twenty-five hundred." He had the receipt to prove the original quote at five thousand, and was ready to find it when Marcus held up a hand.

"Like I said in the beginning, jobs have a tendency to change. This one was more work than I thought. So, price changed too."

"Then why didn't you tell me that before you finished? If the job and price changed, then you should have told me so I could have decided what to do."

Marcus continued packing his things. "Either way, you would have had to agree. The work needed to be done, or the house wouldn't be safe to live in."

"That's not how this works," Augustus argued. "You've always let me know when jobs changed in the past."

"Look, the price is the price. If you don't want to pay it, I'm more than happy to go up there and take back the cost of what's left in materials. I'd rather not make this messier than it has to be."

Nothing short of shock accompanied the silence Augustus fell into. For a moment he could only stare across the kitchen at the man he'd once thought of as honest and loyal. But, no, Marcus was just another snake lying in wait, ready to rip people off when they already were giving everything they had.

He doesn't deserve his riches. The voice from the bank returned, creeping across his thoughts as though they were his own. *Take from him what he seeks to steal from you.*

"What's it gonna be, Jones?"

Make him believe in fortune that does not exist. The command gave Augustus a strength he didn't know he had. And, though he knew it was wrong, he found himself replying, "I already paid you." The words came out in the raspy tone he heard in the bank. Not his voice, but something...other.

Marcus didn't seem to notice, or didn't care, as he responded, "Yeah, the deposit. Now I need the rest. Four thousand."

No, came the voice, instructing him what to say. *I gave you full payment already. I—*

"—owe you nothing," Augustus finished, his voice hard and stare firm. "Our business here is done, as previously agreed upon."

For a second, he thought Marcus was going to argue—why wouldn't he, Augustus figured. His words were one giant lie and anyone with half a brain would see right through it, especially considering how much money was involved. Except, Marcus didn't. He merely muttered an embarrassed apology and gathered his tools, heading out the front door a few moments later.

Only when he was sure Marcus's truck had pulled out of the driveway did Augustus release the breath he'd been holding. It was a breath filled with anxiety, his heart beginning to race and his hands shaking as they pushed through his hair.

"What the hell is happening to me?" he whispered, trying to determine if he was going insane, or if everyone around him was.

There was one person who might have some answers, though he risked losing her completely if he was actually honest. Deciding it was worth a shot, he pulled out his phone and dialed.

CHAPTER 14

"Why did you call me here, Augustus? It's getting late and we both have tours tonight." Mel let herself into the house, her shout finding Augustus in the kitchen. He waited for her to track him down rather than call back to her, and when she entered, she saw him sitting at the counter, head in his hands.

"Augustus? Are you okay?" Her annoyed tone changed to one of concern. Approaching him, she placed a gentle hand on his shoulder and nudged him until he looked up. "What's going on? Is it your mom? Is she okay?"

"Mom is fine. Probably coming home tomorrow or the day after."

"Then what's wrong?"

"I don't know," he replied honestly. "But you're the only person I know who might be able to help."

Sobered now, all traces of irritation vanished from her expression, Mel sat on the stool next to her friend and took him in. "Okay, now you're scaring me. Augustus Jones is the smooth and suave ghost tour guide, not the scared dude in need of a shower. What's wrong? I've barely seen you since our date and you seem... different."

He'd been thinking of ways to tell her just that, and every explanation just made him sound crazy. Which, maybe he was, but he didn't want Mel to think that from the get-go. "Okay. I need to tell you something, but I'm worried how you are going to take it because I don't want to scare you off. So just listen and have an open mind, okay?"

"Okay," she said slowly, unsurely.

Not able to meet her eyes, Augustus made his confession. "Something weird is happening, and I can't figure out if I'm just losing my mind or if everyone around me is playing some huge joke. It's like…it's like anything I say, people automatically believe."

Mel frowned. "Um…What do you mean?"

"I mean, they *believe* me. I was on a tour a few days ago and said something completely stupid about a historical figure as a joke, and people believed me, no questions asked."

"So? We're the guides. People always believe us because they assume we know what we're talking about." The doubt in her voice was clear, further frustrating him.

"Yeah, but then my contractor tried to rip me off, so I lied and told him I'd already paid him, when really I still owed him money. A lot of money. But he believed me and just packed up and left, without actually getting full payment." He wasn't willing to tell her about the bank yet, and the extra money still sitting in his account. "And to top it off, this creepy bird keeps showing up wherever I go. It doesn't do anything except stare at me in this really weird way."

Mel listened thoughtfully, hands clasped in front of her and brow furrowed. "Okay," she said again, just as slowly. "So a bird is following you, people on a tour believed a lie, and you lied to a contractor about paying him and he didn't question it…. Is there any chance you actually did pay him and just forgot?"

"Not even a small one. It was a large amount. I don't get it." He sighed for what felt like the thousandth time in the past week. "And worse, with the contractor, it was like there was some voice in my head telling me what to say, how to get away with not paying. Before that, I randomly found a ruby in the grass. Oh, and I've been having these awful dreams. One of them was this hideous snake-haired woman who was convinced I wanted revenge on my father. The other had this beast-looking creature who destroyed my old neighborhood, also convinced I wanted my dad dead. Both times I felt like they were trying to get me to agree with them, and when I argued, they disappeared. But it hasn't stopped this weird sudden ability to lie and have people believe me."

For a long moment, Mel only stared at him. He tried reading her expression, but her face was effectively blank of emotion outside of curiosity. Finally, she spoke, her words laced with interest, "Augustus, that all sounds kinda crazy, but also scary. I mean, that's a power that could be easily abused."

"Wait." He held up a hand. "Are you saying you believe me?" Then he realized what he'd just said and shook his head. "Of course you do. Everyone believes me lately, so why wouldn't you believe something completely impossible I just told you?"

"Or maybe I'm a bigger believer in crazy things than you are," she countered. "I remember you asking me about the old voodoo rituals and stories of Savannah the other day. Even then I thought it was weird since you never cared about that stuff before. But it makes sense now, if what you're saying is true, like, maybe you think something supernatural is going on. To me it doesn't sound *too* serious yet. I mean, it was only a couple times and there were no real consequences, but of course I believe you. Why would you lie to me?"

Augustus sighed. The conversation would go nowhere if she just blindly accepted everything he said. "I was kind of hoping you would have ideas about what's going on, not just take everything I say at face value, like the other day."

The words slipped out before he could stop them, and any hope of her letting them go was dashed when her eyes narrowed. "What do you mean, the other day?"

Knowing he was busted, and still feeling weird enough about his newfound ability that he wanted to be honest, he replied,

"When I told you that you said you wanted to go on that date. You never said that. I just said it was a joke and you believed me."

Hurt was apparent on her face, in her tone, when she replied, "Are you saying you tricked me into going out with you?"

"No," he said quickly. "I mean…well, yeah, I suppose I did. But it wasn't intentional, I promise. That was the first time I realized what happened and was so surprised I just kind of went with it."

"You went with it," she repeated quietly. "Is this a joke, Augustus?"

The question caught him off-guard. "What do you mean?"

"I *remember* that conversation, Augustus." Her tone had an urgency to it now. "I remember us in the storage unit, you asking me out again. I remember feeling bad because I'd turned you down so many times, and I remember actually feeling jealous when you mentioned another woman wanting to go out with you." One hand clutched at her chest. "I can still feel those feelings. It was real, Augustus. And now you're trying to tell me it was all a lie?"

Desperation was thick in the air. Augustus wanted to comfort her, but didn't know how. "I don't know what I'm saying, Mel. I don't know how you remember all those things, because *I* don't. What I remember is me asking you on a date and you shooting me down, and me saying you'd regret it when I was famous. There was never another woman. You never agreed to a date. That was the lie. So I don't understand how you can remember something that never happened."

Tears glistened in Mel's eyes as she slid off the stool and grabbed her bag. "I think I understand," she said around a sniffle. "You finally got your date and realized I wasn't what you wanted after all, so now you're trying to make *me* feel like the crazy one."

"No, that's not it at all, Mel. I—"

"Don't. I have to go."

"Mel, wait. I—"

"I'll see you later," she interrupted, all but running out of the kitchen and house, leaving Augustus even more confused and desperate and alone. He jumped off the stool to follow, racing through the open front door, stumbling to a stop on the front porch.

Mel was gone, having already disappeared either on foot or in a car, he wasn't sure. But in her place was the stork, standing in the middle of the narrow sidewalk leading to the porch. From the front step, Augustus watched it, feeling a rock building in the pit of his stomach.

This bird. It wasn't a coincidence. He knew that now. The stork wanted something, expected something out of him.

"What do you want?" he asked, immediately feeling like a fool for talking to a goddamn bird. The stork didn't answer, but didn't move either. Augustus looked left and right, seeing an old and empty clay planter on the railing, and grabbed it. He lifted an arm to throw it at the bird, but when he glanced back at the sidewalk, it was gone.

"Are you fucking kidding me?" he whispered, lowering his arm and dropping the planter at his feet, not noticing when it broke into five jagged pieces. A few quick steps had him down the porch and standing in the same spot as the bird, searching his sides and finding nothing out of the ordinary. His hands went to his head, tugging at his hair.

"I'm losing my fucking mind." But, even as he spoke the words, he knew it wasn't true. It wasn't his mind he was losing, but something else. He just didn't know what.

CHAPTER 15

His ghost tour began at eleven that night. It was a larger group than usual—Sonny's doing, booking as many guests as possible after the apparent success of their new history tours. Augustus had only led two, Voodoo and Mel one each, and Silas on the schedule for several next week, but even those few tours had been enough to stir more business.

His group, as always, met at Colonial Park Cemetery. And, as always, the tourists were in a tight cluster, wary of being out so late at night despite all the activity bustling around them, nervous being at the entrance of a cemetery with gates padlocked at sundown.

"Good evening, brave travelers of my fine Savannah city," he greeted with a cheer he didn't feel, his Irish accent out in full force and accenting his preferred "costume" of flowing white shirt, black coat with popped collar, and thick, buckled boots. Tonight he'd added more rings than usual and a few long necklaces strategically draped over his shirt, which was open at the top despite the chill in the air. He knew he looked good, and his ego always helped him lay on the charm during tours. "Are we ready to explore the nefarious history as midnight looms upon us?"

As the tourists chuckled to themselves and shifted anxiously from foot to foot, Augustus quickly took roll. A few were people from his day tours, but the rest were new to him. He was thankful there were no kids this time so he could say whatever he wanted and not have to worry about keeping an eye out for them, though there was one young woman in the back whose stare on him was even, calculated, and, if he was being honest with himself, a little creepy.

Ready to get started, Augustus asked with his now-famous accent, "Does anyone know why we begin our tour here at Colonial Park Cemetery?" When no one responded, he continued, "This cemetery is home to some of Savannah's darkest tales. Young men buried alive. Bodies exhumed and moved, and, my personal favorite, voodoo rituals performed at midnight."

"What kind of rituals?"

The question came from the woman in the back. Augustus peered through the darkness at her, sensing familiarity but not enough to remember who she was. Her hair was long and dark, almond-shaped eyes watching him curiously, lithe body poised in a strangely prim and proper way. He knew her from somewhere, he was sure of it, but his brain couldn't put the pieces together.

"Satanic rituals," he finally answered her. "The cemetery used to be open to the public day and night, but police and city officials kept finding bodies of dead goats among the tombstones, and other animals that had been sacrificed. But most gruesome of all was the fact that all of these sacrificed animals were missing one thing—their hearts."

He let that sink in, seeing lips curl in disgust, hands clutch at a significant other's. Except for the woman in the back. One corner of her mouth lifted in a smirk as she crossed her arms. "Why the hearts?"

"Because," he said with an arm gesturing to the cemetery, "when you consume the heart of a thing, you are granted its power."

"Sounds fascinating." Her lips curled into a smile, even as the other tourists looked at her in disdain.

"As are all things about this great city, lass," Augustus replied smoothly. He was used to people trying to upstage him, though usually it came from a younger man who had a little too much to drink and wanted to impress the girl he was with. "But tonight isn't about stories that come from the cemetery. Tonight, we explore the people who made Savannah what it is today, and some of the most haunted houses in the United States."

So he led them on their tour, breezing through questions about Jason Waters and Yellow Fever, thoroughly satisfied by his performance so far that night. His crowd was enraptured with his every word. The feeling of adoration and empowerment put an extra spring in his step as he walked them down the street.

"And our last stop of the night, the site I know you've all been waiting for, the infamous house on Abercorn Street."

Before he could say anything else, his most curious tourist asked, "Can you tell us the story of Tessa Taylor?"

Augustus eyed the woman. She'd remained in the back the entire tour, not saying a word since her first question at the cemetery, giving each site a careful once-over but never appearing too interested. Now, though, he had her full attention.

"The story of Tessa Taylor," he repeated, deciding to answer the question like he did every other time it was asked. He stood with his back to the house. There was nothing he wanted less than to look at the home and risk seeing something he would never get out of his head.

"Tessa, her best friend, and her fiancé joined me for a tour about two years ago. She was a pleasant enough young woman. A little jumpy, but how many of you aren't?" He smiled teasingly, getting a few grins out of the crowd. "Our tour went as all tours do—a little spooky, a lot of fun. But it was after visiting this very house behind me that her fiancé, Ben, noticed Tessa and her friend were missing."

He remembered how worried he'd been. That had been the first time anyone in his group ever went missing, though he'd never have imagined it was because they went into the house. He would have preferred it if they got lost or fell back due to an injury.

"The group and I backtracked to the house on Abercorn, and by the time we rounded the corner, Tessa and her friend were on the sidewalk. Now, at the time, no one knew what they had done. It wasn't until a couple weeks later that they came to see me, revealing the truth of that night."

Sure, he'd always suspected Tessa and Kerry went into the house, but he hadn't had the evidence to accuse him. And, even if he did, it wouldn't have served any purpose except to let them know they were both a major pain in the ass.

"Tessa spoke to me of nightmares, of strange voices in her head, of a constant feeling of being watched. Something was after her, she said, and feared something supernatural had happened to her in the house."

It was more or less the truth, with some liberties taken.

"To be honest, I thought she was just a dramatic girl who needed help I wasn't able to give. I didn't see her after that, not until news stories broke of her escaping the hospital after attacking her former boss, Jason Waters. The things that happened between our last meeting and her escape, I can't say. All I know is that Tessa Taylor entered that house, and when she came out, she was a completely different woman. One who developed a sudden interest in murdering child abusers."

"And was Tessa really possessed? Is something demonic happening in that house?"

The question made his stomach flutter in fear. There was no doubt in his mind that something was happening inside that house, but hell if he would tell any of these people that. They were clearly freaked out enough, and the last thing he needed was more tourists getting it in their heads that they needed to go exploring.

"No." His voice was firm, a bit cold even, unnatural-sounding to him. "There is nothing supernatural about the house. It's just an old house with a bad past."

His lie resonated with the people, who visibly relaxed as he spoke. With his final declaration, he led the group back to the cemetery, accepting their tips and praises as each tourist left. Soon only the woman was left.

She approached him with a smile, holding a hand out to shake. "A wonderful tour as always, Augustus Jones."

He accepted her hand, his mind working hard to place her; still, he found nothing in his memories of her face, her voice. Had it of been any other woman, he would have flirted a little, but this one creeped him out despite the tug in his chest that almost made him feel like they were old friends. "I appreciate it. Glad you had a good time."

"Oh, I did." She pulled back her arm and made to turn away, pausing to add, "Funny how they believe anything you say, isn't it?" Then she winked and walked away, leaving Augustus staring after her, mouth parted.

Only then did he realize his hand wasn't empty. He looked down, somehow not surprised to see the red stone laying in his palm. Glancing back up, he saw the woman was gone. "I'm in deep shit," he muttered, and that same sense of dread followed him home.

CHAPTER 16

Determined to get a few hours' sleep before he had to pick his mother up from the hospital, Augustus went straight to bed when he got home, not bothering with a shower. He glanced at his phone before plugging it in, noting it was just after 1 AM.

"Witching hour is upon us," he said to himself, settling down. Immediately his thoughts went to the woman during his tour. Who the hell was she? What did she mean by people believing anything he said? There was no way she could know what was happening with him. But then, why did she give him the ruby?

He'd set the stone on the nightstand, next to the other one. They were about the same size, and he wondered how much they were worth. Maybe tomorrow he'd stop by the pawn shop before going to the hospital, see if they were even real.

Enough, he silently ordered himself. Closing his eyes, Augustus willed his body to sleep.

His dream took him to a secluded place, a forest filled with brilliant greens and browns and yellows. A warm and welcoming environment, inviting him to walk upon a path not often traveled. Looking down, he saw two sets of footprints set in a sandy path, both leading to the same place—a stone altar in the middle of a clearing.

Augustus followed the trail, but stopped at the edge of the clearing. Something didn't feel right. He knew this was a dream, but it felt too familiar to the others he'd had lately, like someone—

some*thing*—was waiting for him at that altar, and he wasn't in a hurry to find out what.

A prick against his leg broke his concentration from the altar. He looked down, a startled gasp escaping when he saw he was dressed in a white suit, crisp and smooth and...feathery soft.

"What the...?" Shaking hands pressed against his chest, down to his waist. Actual feathers. His suit was made of a bird's feathers, beautifully white and clean. More white feathers were strewn about the ground, leading to the stone altar. With a sigh, Augustus resumed his trek, stepping up on the enormous rock and seeing just what was waiting for him.

"Fuck," he muttered when he saw the bloody body of a dying stork laying on the stone. He fell to his knees, ends of the feathers stabbing into his skin, and reached out to the bird. Its back was raw, feathers plucked from tender flesh, puncture wounds oozing blood. Beady black eyes gazed up at him weakly, tear-like moisture leaking down to its beak, which was pale and cracked. It was a tortured gaze, and he hated to think of the pain the poor creature had been dealt in its final moments.

"Sorry, buddy. I certainly would never have asked for a suit of your feathers." Sure, he'd never been much of a pet person, but he hated to see innocent animals suffer. "I'd take your pain away if I could."

With his words, Augustus became excruciatingly aware of the feathers against his skin, their sharp ends scraping against him. He winced, trying to adjust the suit away from those tender areas, but the quills dug in deeper, stabbing him all over, blood starting to seep through and stain the white.

Augustus cried out in pain, hands pulling at the surprisingly strong suit that refused to break or tear, just as the stork began to laugh. It was an awful, raucous, unnatural sound that filled the clearing and exploded into Augustus's ears with a screeching blast. And, with its laugh, it began to change.

Skinny legs elongated, cracking and bending and growing with hard brown flesh. The raw and bloody back stretched into a torso with protruding ribs and spine, snapping into a body six feet tall. The body roughly resembled a man, deformed and sickly but a man nonetheless. But the face—Augustus saw with horror it was not a human face at all.

The broken beak had grown, stretching out from a roughly lined jaw. Round, black eyes stared at him from above the beak, and below a forehead lined with thick nodules. There was nothing gentle or soft about this creature, which now stood before him naked, though its flesh seemed to have regrown a thin feathered coating.

Before Augustus could say anything, the wind began to blow, casting him in darkness until all he could see was the stone beneath his feet and the beast in front of him. The trees, the grass, the clearing, it all had disappeared. In its place, a red glow surrounded them, reminding him of Hell.

The creature moved, first holding up a hand, showing Augustus a finger tipped with a deadly sharp nail. Then it lowered, bending at the waist and walking a slow circle around the man, who stood perfectly still, afraid that any move would send that nail through his heart.

The scratch of nail against rock grated against his nerves, and only when it stopped did Augustus let out the breath burning in his chest. His eyes moved down to see what the bird-like beast had done, and he saw he stood in the middle of a triangle etched deep into the altar.

Countless stories he'd told during ghost tours came rushing back at him. Stories about sacrifices and spells and offerings to the darkness by cult leaders who'd set up camp in the cemetery. He didn't know what a triangle signified, but there was no doubt this was meant to be a ritual, and he was the sacrifice. Without looking at the nightmarish bird, Augustus made to leap off the rock and race away from his almost certain death, but an unseen force kept his feet rooted in place.

"Shit," he cursed vehemently, his teeth clenched with the effort. The harder he tried to escape, the more the quills dug into his skin, and the more the beast laughed. The rough, garbled sound filled him with trepidation.

"How odd that you all try to escape, those who find themselves within my presence, without ever learning the truth of where you stand." The voice reminded Augustus of stones being crushed. And, worse, it reminded him of the way his own sounded the few times he'd gotten away with his lies. "Where once I was bound, now you stand."

Augustus attempted to appear confident, fearless, and was sure he failed miserably, if the creature's baleful stare was any indication. How it managed to appear amused and bored and annoyed all at the same time baffled him.

Knowing intimidation was pointless, Augustus gave up and instead asked, "Who are you?"

Now its expression turned to insult. The creature held its arms out and offered a bow. But no, Augustus saw, not quite arms. Limbs, covered with bloody feathers that stretched to the ground, most of them broken or frayed. "I am the commander of the thirty legions," it replied with an air of authority. "I am the high duke of Hell. I am the one they call Shax."

When Augustus didn't reply, his own expression making it clear he had no idea who or what Shax was, the beast edged closer. Its beak pressed against Augustus's cheek. "And what do they call you, the unbeliever who stands upon my altar?"

His skin burned and the words stuck in his throat as he spoke them. "I'm, um, Augustus. Augustus Jones."

The air turned cold, sending a chill down Augustus's spine. The demon who called itself Shax edged even closer to whisper in his ear, "And what treasures do you desire, dear Augustus Jones?"

"Treasures?" he repeated, instantly thinking back to the two rubies next to his bed. He did want more of those. Or did the demon mean some other kind of treasure?

"Treasures….The things that call to your heart most." Shax began to circle Augustus, watching him closely. Those long, feathered arms clasped behind its back, forcing a rigid and authoritative posture that reminded the man of his mystery tourist earlier in the night. "What is it you desire most?"

There were many things he desired—money, a new house, his mother's improved health, a second chance with Mel—but the beast seemed to be looking for one specific answer. Augustus had a feeling that if he answered incorrectly, it would not end favorably for him. So instead of giving an answer, he replied, "I…I guess it depends on what exactly you're looking for."

"Shall I help you?" Shax stopped in front of him, lifting one of those fingers again and placing it against his forehead. The nail dug into his flesh. Augustus could imagine it pulling memories out of his head, could feel it doing just that as the creature searched through thirty-five years of history.

"Perhaps you desire a painful death for your father. Ah, yes, the man who caused you such harm, your mother such misery." There was no mockery in its tone, a voice merely stating the facts.

"Perhaps you desire a new home fit for a king. Yes, you live in such squalor now, not a home fit for the man you have become." Again it was a monotone comment, yet even still made Augustus feel less of a man.

"Or perhaps you desire all the riches of the world, even if you have to steal them from every man and woman you meet. Enough riches to earn you the woman you love, the home you desire, the lifestyle you crave."

It was with no small amount of horror Augustus realized he did want all those things. It wasn't hard to imagine himself as a wealthy man, in a huge home filled with beautiful decorations and the staff to take care of them. Just as it was easy to see himself at his father's funeral. Yes, he would go, if only to make sure the man was actually dead.

But to admit those things out loud was a step he wasn't yet willing to take, especially to a demon invading his dreams—a demon who very well could have been a figment of his imagination. In that moment, Augustus thought up a lie. Surely the beast would believe him. Everyone believed his lies lately.

He would tell the demon that what he desired most was for his mother to be healthy, to have her mind back. It was true, he really did want that almost as much as the other things, so he hoped the lie would appease the creature. Augustus opened his mouth to speak, the words on the tip of his tongue, but he choked before any sound came out. His breath stuck in his throat, suffocating him.

Augustus dropped to his knees, hands clawing at his throat as it constricted. The demon hovered over him with a mocking laugh. "Only the truth, my dear Augustus Jones. In this triangle, only the truth can be spoken, lest you choke on your own deceits."

The invisible hand around his neck loosened, letting in tiny slivers of air Augustus gulped up. With a coarse cough, he rose on shaky legs, ready to speak the truth if it meant getting the hell out of here and back to the real world. "Okay," he rasped out, holding up a hand. Shax stepped back, waiting patiently to hear the truth.

"The greatest treasure I desire is…fame and wealth, and everything that comes with it." It felt selfish and egotistical to say it out loud, but the demon nodded, motioning for him to continue. "I want people to know and praise my name. I want to be rich and never have to worry about paying bills again. I want a good house for me, and for my mother. I want to be in a place where people know better than to rip me off. I want to be Augustus Jones. Not Nathaniel Jones."

The Shax beast smiled, a grotesque grin on a cracked beak. "No," it rumbled, "not Nathaniel Jones. Why would you want to be Nathaniel, when you could be Augustus Jones, the wealthiest man in town?"

"Exactly." He wanted it. The desire to have money burned within him. He'd grown up with nothing, courtesy of a father who'd rather drink it all away. Now he wanted everything he'd always been denied.

"Such lofty goals," the demon whispered thoughtfully. "I can give you the treasures your heart desires. All you have to do, dear one, is take them."

The red glow around them began to glitter. Augustus looked around to find the grass surrounding the altar was strewn with gold and gemstones. Reds and greens and golds sparkled, reflecting on the altar in a kaleidoscope of color. And he wanted them. Every single one, so much so his fingers twitched and perverse pleasure flooded through him at the very thought of touching them.

Turning back to the beast, Augustus held his head high. His voice was confident and even when he replied, "Give them to me."

CHAPTER 17

Augustus slept soundly that night, his dreams moving into visions of what his future could be like should he be given everything he ever wanted. It was a life filled with comfort, his every need provided for, where women wanted to be with him, and men wanted to be him. He was Augustus Jones, more than just a ghost tour guide. Successful businessman, charitable community member, famous and infamous alike for his knowledge of all things spooky.

When he awoke, it was with a smile on his face. Even if those things never happened anywhere outside of his dreams, it was a nice thought to get him started each morning.

"Shax," he said to himself as he dressed for the day in jeans and a button-down shirt, his usual attire on his rare days off. Part of him wanted to run straight to the computer and look up the supposed demon, see if he was real or just another figment of his imagination. But another part didn't want to know. He wanted the fantasy, however short-lived it would be, *needed* to believe something better was coming, even if it was at the hands of an evil spirit who dressed him in a feather suit.

His first stop on the way to the hospital was the pawn shop. The two rubies were burning a hole in his pocket and he could already smell the money he'd get from them. Any little bit would help, and be immediately put toward a new house.

"Morning, Jones," Charles, the shop owner, greeted him when he entered. The two knew each other from several trades in the past when Augustus needed extra cash. Charles was one of the few people Augustus trusted, though after the ordeal with the contractor, he was a little hesitant. "What ya got for me today?"

"Not sure," Augustus replied honestly. At the counter, he placed the gemstones in front of the old man. "Mom had these in an old jewelry box. Doesn't want them, so I figured I'd see what I could get out of them."

Charles slid the rubies across the counter while frowning over at the other man. "You sick?" At Augustus's furrowed brow, he added, "Your voice. Sounds different."

"Oh, yeah, had back-to-back tours yesterday. Lost my voice a little." He couldn't explain why he sounded like the demon man-bird from his dreams, and didn't want to try. It was easier to lie.

"Augustus Jones, always working," the shop owner commented as he inspected the gemstones, pulling a small magnifying glass from somewhere behind the counter and holding it and a ruby up to his eye. Augustus knew the older man was certified in gemstone authentication, which was one reason why he'd brought them here.

After a moment, Charles let out a low whistle. "Augustus, these are the real deal." He held one up to the light, admiring it with an appreciation only someone who truly knew what he was looking at could show. "These are worth some money, more than I can give you. You're better off taking them to a jeweler."

"No. I'll take whatever you can give me."

Charles lowered the stone and eyed the guide, the response raising suspicion. But Augustus knew he wouldn't press the matter. That was the point of the shop—sell, trade, buy, and never ask questions.

"I can't give you fair marketing value," Charles relented, holding both stones in the palm of his hand, "but we can work out a deal."

You don't make deals, said the Shax spirit in his head. *You take what you want, what you deserve.*

But Augustus wasn't willing to take from the man he'd known for nearly fifteen years, especially when he'd been nothing but honest the entire transaction. So instead of creating a lie, he simply said, "Make your best offer."

*

He walked out of the pawn shop a thousand dollars richer and with a smirk of satisfaction on his face. Sure, he could have gotten more out of the trade, but considering he paid nothing for the rubies, he had no complaints.

As he drove to the hospital, he thought of all the ways he could spend the money. Maybe a nice dinner at his mother's favorite restaurant, or a trip for him and Mel, assuming she was willing to give him another shot. Or perhaps he'd put it all in savings in preparation of buying a home.

So many possibilities floated through his mind the entire drive, and as he walked through the hospital to his mother's room. She was being discharged within the hour and couldn't wait a second longer.

"Nathaniel!" she all but cheered when he entered. Already she was attempting to dress herself and move from the bed.

He rushed to her side, as did the nurse and doctor. "Easy, Mom. We'll get you out of there soon, don't you worry. But I need to finalize the paperwork first."

"Well, get to it! I've got shows to catch up on and a nap to enjoy in my nice, comfy bed." She smiled over at him, the joy in finally getting to go home apparent in her eyes.

"Mr. Jones, can I have a word before we get the discharge papers?" Dr. Bart Wells asked, gesturing to Augustus, who nodded and followed him out the door.

"Is there a problem with my mother being released today?" he asked after they had come to a stop in the hallway around the corner from Gert's room. The look of concern on Dr. Wells's face had his heart skipping a beat.

Glancing down at his clipboard, Dr. Wells replied, "No, she can be released today. But I wanted to discuss with you her future care." At Augustus's frown, he continued, "One of my nurses noticed your mother was experiencing some confusion at certain times during the day. Once she forgot what they were discussing mid-conversation. Another time she forgot why she was in the hospital and panicked. Have you experienced this with her recently?"

He wanted to say no, to lie to himself and say everything was fine, but in this moment he needed to know the truth. "Yes," he admitted, crestfallen. "For about four or five months now. It started with little things, forgetting what she had for breakfast, or that she had plans with a friend. Nothing to really cause worry. But lately it's been getting worse. It's why she ended up here in the first place. She forgot we had discussed me getting the roof fixed, and for some reason took it upon herself to try to repair it."

"I see." The doctor nodded, scribbling a few notes down on his chart. "Mr. Jones, I'm sorry to say, but I think your mother is experiencing early signs of Alzheimer's."

He'd suspected just that, but it still pained him to hear it said out loud, by a doctor no less. Swallowing hard, Augustus replied, "Truth be told, I was wondering the same thing. I guess I was hoping for a miracle and things would just get better." Dr. Wells didn't reply, so he asked, "What do we do now?"

"Now, you take your mother home and make her comfortable. Her body has been through a lot but her healing is looking good. As for the other issue, right now the best thing to do is just keep your eye on her. Depending on how things progress, you might want to consider looking into long-term care options, possibly even a home with staff who are trained to deal with Alzheimer's patients."

A home was the last thing he'd ever do to his mother, but Augustus didn't tell the doctor that. He just nodded and listened to instructions for her care, then handled the rest of the paperwork needed to get her home.

CHAPTER 18

"All right, Mom. You stay right here, get some rest, and I'll make you some tea."

Augustus made sure Gert was settled in the recliner chair—she'd refused the bed, claiming she needed some time off a mattress before giving in to a nap—then set the television to play the shows he'd recorded on the DVR. She'd be entertained for the next several hours between the TV, her crosswords, and the snacks he would soon be placing on the table next to the chair.

"You are a wonderful son," Gert gushed, pulling a thick blanket over her legs with her good arm. "My wonderful Nathaniel."

"Mom. How many times have I told you, my name is Augustus?" He didn't wait for her answer, realizing only when he reached the kitchen that he'd just told her a lie. Would she believe it? Would she now know him only as Augustus Jones, and be given new memories to accommodate the lie?

He didn't want to find out. Not now, when she was so fragile already, her mind at its breaking point. *No more lying to her*, he promised himself. Even if she called him Nathaniel, he wouldn't argue.

Augustus made quick work of getting her snacks and tea, ensuring Gert was comfortable before retreating to his bedroom. He'd taken a few days off to take care of her, and planned on using the time to make sense of his new and entirely baffling world.

From the surface of his dresser, an old and battered laptop beckoned. Augustus grabbed it with one hand and set it on the bed, waiting impatiently for the ancient computer to boot up and, miraculously, actually connect to the wireless signal. Once Google was opened, he began his search.

First he typed in *Shax*, hoping the single word would yield him a wealth of answers. Instead he found a bunch of websites talking about a television show featuring a trio of witches. He'd watched a few episodes here and there just so he could relate to the comments and questions brought up by the younger generation during tours, but the show never really caught his interest.

Trying again, he typed *Shax demon*. "Here we go," he muttered, reading the first result that brought up a list of demons by name.

"The Shax," he read off the page, unblinking eyes scanning the long paragraphs. "The Great Marquis of Hell, known for his power over thirty legions of demons on dark, supernatural horses. The Shax is a skilled trickster, able to take away the sight and hearing of any person under his spell, as well as twist their minds until they no longer know who they are."

Augustus ran a hand through his hair. "Freaky." So far, the information didn't completely match what he knew of the alleged demon that visited him in sleep, but it was still unnerving.

"The demon is also known for stealing fortune from others. Stories are told of the Shax stealing money from the palaces of kings and giving it back to the people it was taken from. He rarely steals for himself, instead being tasked to steal by the one who conjures him."

Conjures? As far as Augustus knew, he hadn't done any conjuring lately.

"More than a clever thief, the Shax is good at finding lost treasures. He is known to discover hidden things, money and jewels long since forgotten." Now it was starting to sound familiar. It wasn't until the weird dreams began that Augustus started finding rubies and twenty-dollar bills just laying on the ground for him to find. As though they had been hidden, only to be discovered by the one who knew where to find all things lost.

Scrolling farther down the page, Augustus forced himself to keep reading. "The Shax demon is faithful to the one it serves and the world in which it lives, but will lie and deceive when necessary to ensure its good fortune continues. The only way to ensure the truth is spoken is to capture the demon in a...." Here his voice trailed off, breath hitching in his throat, before he managed a whispered, "*Triangle*."

For a moment, Augustus could only hang his head, tears pricking the corners of his eyes. It was real, too real, the facts too closely aligned to his dream and the things happening in his waking hours for him to deny the coincidence. Never in his life had he heard about the Shax, so there was no way he could have been pulling from memories and call it a simple nightmare.

Still, he forced himself to keep reading.

"Only when the Shax is forced into the triangle will he speak beautifully all the truths the conjurer or exorcist wants to know, including the location of riches and treasures. If he escapes the triangle, he will once again deceive, taking with him all the truths of the world's wealth and fortunes."

The last line brought Augustus to the end of the page. His eyes moved from the final word—*fortunes*—to the picture, an artistic rendering of what the author supposed the demon looked like. While the drawing looked nothing like the beast he'd seen in his dreams, it still have him chills. The beady black eyes, the stork's head on a man's body, the great arching wings much more beautiful than the dingy ones of the real Shax....

Real Shax? he repeated to himself, wondering when he'd decided this whole thing was actually happening. *Was* he accepting the fact that a demon was trying to, what? Seduce him? Pull him over to the dark side?

"I said I wanted it," he remembered, piecing together bits of the dream. The spirit offered him the world and he took it—what did that mean?

A knock at the front door pulled Augustus from his research. Words like *high marquis* and *silver* and *treasures* rang in his head. It had to be some sick twist of fate, all these dreams coming to him, rubies appearing, voices in his head; all of it happening at once had to be for a reason. He still wasn't ready to believe it was because an actual demon had found him or was promising to give him all the treasures he desired.

A camera light flashed in his face as soon as he opened the door. Augustus blinked and stumbled back a step, instantly pissed off. "What the hell is wrong with you?"

"Mr. Jones! What can you tell us about the new Beware! ghost tour company?"

Frozen in place by the sight of so many reporters and cameramen camped out on his front yard, Augustus could only stare. It didn't make sense, all these people wanting to talk to him about some company he'd never even heard of.

"Mr. Jones!" the woman said again, a smile plastered on her pretty face. "Any comments on how you plan to take Savannah's most popular ghost tour company and make it your own?"

Searching for his voice, Augustus managed a weak, "Um... what?"

The reporter smiled, though her eyes told a different reaction. Still, she was pleasant as she repeated herself. "What can you tell us about the new Beware! ghost tour company?"

What the hell is that? he asked himself, searching his mind for the name, and for any reason why the woman would think he was "making it his own." But he didn't want to look like a moron on camera, so he refused to ask. "Well, what do you want to know?"

Now her smile and eyes were genuine as she eagerly anticipated a story. The reporter moved next to him, angling them both at the camera. "I'm here with Savannah's own local celebrity turned entrepreneur, Augustus Jones. We all know and love Augustus from his midnight tours, and his more recent daytime history tours around town, and now we have an even more exciting development!" Next she turned to Augustus, who kept his expression neutral while wondering what the clearly delusional woman was talking about.

"I'm sure all your fans are excited to learn you are now operating your own ghost tour company."

I am? But he nodded, turning on his charm as he replied, "The ghost tour business has been good to me. Only made sense to start my own company." He didn't know where the words came from. It felt as though something had overtaken him, giving him an awareness he never knew he had, helping him talk about a life he wasn't living.

"What are your plans for your company, now that you've taken over the company formerly known as Harvest Haunts?"

That threw him. Harvest Haunts was the name of the company he worked for—Sonny's company. The reporter was claiming he took over a business. Did he buy out Sonny? When? Augustus's heart began to pound.

"Um…haven't made too many plans yet," he replied, glad his voice didn't sound as shaky as his body felt. "But now that I'm in charge, you can expect to see great things in the near future." What those things were, he was yet to discover.

"Can you give us any hints about the new Beware! ghost tour company?" she pressed, only to have him shake his head.

"Not yet. Except that, for starters, it's not Beware! ghost tour company. It's just Beware!"

She chuckled, holding the mic up as she asked, "Just the single word? Why Beware as the single word? Does it mean anything?"

Now he grinned too, and the answer escaped before he could think about it. "Yeah. It means, 'Fuckers, beware!'" Both the reporter and the cameraman made a sound of panic and he realized the feed must be live. Their concern only made him grin wider even as his heart beat harder against his chest. That wasn't what he wanted to say, didn't even make sense, yet something inside him was fueling his brain and making his mouth form words he didn't condone.

And, yet, he couldn't stop. "Anyone who goes on my tours knows we travel to the darkest parts of Savannah. They want to be haunted. They want to be scared. But most of them don't realize just what they're asking for. With my company, they're going to know. They're going to be scared. They're going to get up close and personal with terror, one way or another. So my company name makes it clear what they are getting—something they better beware of."

Then he shrugged and leaned against the doorframe, adding, "Then again, if you think you're brave enough, sign up for a tour and get ready for the thrill of a lifetime."

The reporter stared up at him for a second, then schooled her features and turned to the camera. "You heard it here first! Augustus Jones, the man bringing excitement back to Savannah."

When the camera light flashed off, the woman lowered the mic and glared at Augustus. "Thank you for your interview, Mr. Jones. But for future reference, you can't curse like that on live television."

Her scolding instantly angered him. If she hadn't ambushed him at home, and actually requested an interview, he could have been prepared with something more politically correct. But he didn't voice that. Instead he leaned down so he was speaking in her ear, his voice low and rough and not his own.

"The rules have changed, Miss. If you want to make it as a reporter and earn your place in the media, then you better change your language. There is no such thing as being politically correct anymore."

He pulled away, seeing the glaze in her eyes as she processed his statement. With a nod, she slowly walked down the three steps, gesturing for her cameraman to do the same. Not once did she argue or look back, and it wasn't until she reached his mailbox that Augustus saw the stork perched on top of it.

The pounding started again as the interview came back to his now-clear mind. What he'd said. What the reporter claimed he'd done. The lie he'd told. The feeling of something overtaking his body. And the research he'd been doing before the knock at his front door about the demon named Shax.

"What have I done?" he whispered, eyes never leaving the bird. The stork lowered its head as though in a single nod before a scratchy voice entered Augustus's mind.

Taken the first step into your new life, it said. *Embrace the truth only you can create.*

Then the bird fluttered away, leaving Augustus alone with his lies.

CHAPTER 19

He went to the only person who would know what was going on. The only person he'd be able to find, anyway.

The river to his left was smooth as he stalked toward the hospital, a contrast to the chaos swirling within him, though the cold wind coming off the water matched the constant chill freezing his spine. Augustus kept his hands in his pockets and head down until he entered the wide hospital doors. He took only a moment to check the directory before heading up the elevator.

The ride to the top floor seemed to take hours. Every so often it would stop, allowing on a doctor or nurse, occasionally someone dressed in regular clothes. He didn't speak to any of them, choosing to stay at the back and pretend he was invisible. If they spoke to him, he might not be able to stop himself from lying, and wasn't willing to sacrifice the minds and lives of strangers who had done nothing to him.

The elevator finally dinged his arrival. Slowly stepping out, Augustus let the doors slide shut behind him before moving forward, toward the large desk where a receptionist sat. She looked up and smiled at his approach, fluffing her auburn hair over one shoulder. A pretty woman, she was young, with wide green eyes that perfectly complemented her auburn hair, a smooth complexion decorated with entirely too much makeup, and a killer body adorned in a tight black dress.

Augustus had a feeling she was hired based on purely physical attributes.

"Hi," he greeted, leaning against the counter and wondering if a more flirtatious or direct approach would be best. "My name is Augustus Jones. I'm—"

"Augustus Jones!" she interrupted, excitement lighting up her face. "I remember seeing you on the news! I can't wait to take a trip up to Savannah and sign up for one of your tours. It will probably scare me half to death, but it will be worth it."

Flirtatious, he decided, and offered her a half-grin he knew always charmed his female tourists. Though he wasn't wearing his signature pirate-bootlegger-gangster outfit, he still felt confident enough to cock an eyebrow her direction.

"I'll be happy to have you," he replied, and it was the truth. He wouldn't mind looking at her for a couple hours as he walked around Savannah at midnight. "If you get a little spooked, you won't have to worry. I'll be there to protect you."

She blushed and started straightening the items on her desk. A distraction, one he noted and was a little turned on by. "That sounds fun. How, um, how can I help you?"

"I'm here to see Jason Waters."

Her eyes turned to a closed door to her right. Augustus followed her stare, just now noticing the man's name on the opaque glass door. The fact that she looked told him Jason was in there, so he expected her next question.

"Do you have an appointment?"

He almost said no and was prepared to flirt a little more, but then remembered his newfound abilities. Only a moment's hesitation stopped him before he decided one little lie wouldn't hurt her. "Yes, I do. He's expecting me in about five minutes."

The receptionist smiled and stood. He wondered if there was a schedule or book of sorts with a list of appointments, as he noted she didn't bother to double check. "I'll show you in." She led him to the closed office door, knocking twice and listening for a response to enter before turning the handle and taking a single step inside. Augustus stayed at her side, but even from just outside the door he could just barely see the profile of the man who saved Jacksonville from an organ-destroying plague.

"Mr. Waters, Augustus Jones is here for his appointment with you."

If Jason Waters was surprised by the non-existent appointment that brought Augustus to his office, he didn't show it. Instead he merely nodded. "Thank you, Julia. That will be all."

When the young woman closed the door behind her, Augustus took in a deep breath and faced Jason squarely. He hadn't seen him in a long time, and their last meeting had left him confused, and a little scared. The man who stood before him now looked like Jason Waters, sounded like him, but there was a distinct air about him that gave an other-worldly vibe Augustus was just now starting to recognize.

"Augustus," Jason spoke first. "I was wondering when you'd finally come to see me."

The opening hadn't been expected. "What do you mean?"

"You're here for answers, I presume?"

Augustus didn't like the way he asked that. It was too knowing, too calculated, and he had no desire to relive the night Jason was likely talking about. "Well, yes, but probably not about what you're thinking."

Jason walked to a set of chairs by a large window overlooking the river and took a seat, motioning for Augustus to do the same. After a moment, he obeyed. "What do you think I am thinking of?"

Suddenly uncomfortable, Augustus fought not to shift in his chair, pretending to look around the office instead. Only one wall was decorated with a picture of downtown Jacksonville at night, and a plant was sitting in the far corner in front of a tall floor lamp. The desk was facing the river, bare of any items save for the computer. It was a cold office, both in temperature and in atmosphere.

Brought back to the conversation by Jason crossing one ankle over his knee, Augustus replied, "Well, that night. The night you came back to Savannah."

Jason smiled, his handsome face taking on an almost sinister glimmer. "Ah, yes, that was a fun night, wasn't it?"

Fun wasn't a word Augustus would have used to describe that night at all, the night that shook the very foundation of his life and made him question everything he thought he believed in. And, despite his best efforts, he let the memory flood before his eyes.

Augustus left his tour group for the night, bidding them all a safe journey home. It was long past midnight, a time when most scurried home to get out of the shadows, but he basked in it, enjoying the quiet, the gentle chirp of crickets, the sleepiness of his beloved Savannah.

So caught up in enjoying his evening stroll, Augustus didn't notice the dark figure leaning against the cemetery gate until a voice spoke in his ear, "Mr. Jones, we meet again."

Augustus jumped, peering through the night and trying to make out the face of his mysterious visitor. The man stood with one foot propped up against one of the bars, arms crossed, black hat pulled down low over his face. It wasn't until he lifted his head that recognition set in.

"Jason? Jason Waters?" He frowned when the man grinned and pushed himself off the gate. Gone was the limp that had slowed him down during their trek around town less than a month ago. Gone was the pain etched in his every expression with each movement, no matter how slow. In its place was the cool, collected, unaffected mannerisms of a man with not a care in the world.

"What are you doing here? And what are you doing here in the middle of the night?"

Jason pushed his hat back slightly. "Waiting for you, of course."

"Why?" He couldn't hide the suspicion in his voice, nor did he try. There was nothing normal about this scene.

But the lab director didn't seem to notice or care that Augustus held no trust for him. He merely reached back and grabbed hold of the shovel Augustus, who now took a few steps back, had missed earlier. "Relax. I simply need your help."

Augustus eyed the shovel. "For what?"

In one smooth, quick motion, Jason stood before the tour guide, so close he could hear the man's uneasy heartbeat. "For the greatest medical discovery of our time, of course."

Words failed Augustus in that moment. So he merely stood there, watching as Jason slung the shovel over his shoulder and began walking away, keeping close to the cemetery gate. After he'd walked a few paces, he turned back and asked, "Are you coming?"

Curiosity had Augustus moving forward, watching the man carefully. His every step was perfect and pain free—this was not the same Jason Waters he met with before. Something had changed, and it was more than just some aspirin temporarily blocking agonizing scar tissue buildup in a sliced-open gut. Whatever that something was, it gave Jason a terrifying glint to his eyes.

Jason waited until the guide stopped at his side. "I want you to show me where they are buried."

Another glance at the shovel before he repeated, "...Buried?"

"The yellow fever victims. I want to know the exact spot, from end to end."

"Uh...." Augustus peered around, almost hoping for someone to pass by, but the road was strangely empty. It was 2 AM, but typically someone was out at this late hour, whether driving home from a bar, from a tour, or heading to the next party. But the more he looked around, the faster he saw just how silent and still the world was.

Like it was just the two of them in this world, until one got what he wanted from the other.

As though reading his thoughts, Jason cocked his head to the side and offered a small, almost sarcastic smile. The shovel was set against a tree as one hand lifted to grip Augustus's shoulder.

Augustus wanted to step back—then made the mistake of looking into the other man's eyes. In them he saw compassion, intrigue, and...interest. A seductive, dark interest he couldn't look away from. The hand on his shoulder warmed his skin through his clothes, sending that same warmth through his entire body until he began to crave more of it. He felt feverish, but it was a welcomed and nearly orgasmic fever, like his every nerve ending was heating up and exploding simultaneously.

He was lost to the sensation, enough that he didn't notice when Jason pressed himself even closer, their bodies almost molded together. "Imagine it," he whispered, his voice reaching the deepest, darkest parts of Augustus. "Imagine the discoveries we can make together, a historian with all the knowledge of a past world, a medical professional with the skill to transform an ancient virus, the entire world speaking our names and reveling in our power."

Augustus saw it as Jason spoke—a future where they were celebrated, where the spotlight was focused only on them for the parts they played in transforming science as the world knew it. He wanted it, more than he'd ever wanted anything, and he didn't even know what it was.

"Tell me what you need," Augustus whispered back. There was desperation in his voice, building with each touch. He felt the hand on his shoulder slide up to his throat, warm fingers taking hold before traveling across his chest.

"You know what I need." This was said firmly, enough so that Augustus opened his eyes—not realizing they'd even been closed as he basked in the feverish sensation—and focused on Jason. For one confusing, fleeting moment, Augustus wanted him, all of him, pressed up against the cemetery gate, the two of them indulging in their most carnal desires. But just as quickly as the wanting washed over him, it passed, leaving in its wake an unwavering determination to give this man everything he asked for.

So Augustus slid away from his touch and led Jason to the cracked slab of concrete that once served as a basketball court for neighborhood kids. Beneath that concrete lay the bones of yellow fever victims in one of many mass graves dug during a time when too many died with too little left to care for them.

He marked one spot with a rock, then walked to the other end and placed a second marker. "End to end," he told Jason, then gestured to the large oak tree separating the concrete from the sidewalk and road. "And the tree, growing at the head of the trench. Of course, this is all just speculation. You realize that, right? The things we say in our tours, sometimes it's just to spook people."

A chuckle rumbled out of Jason as he nodded. "Oh yes, I understand the value of your ghost tour, Mr. Jones. But we both know which stories have truth to them, don't we?"

Choosing not to reply, Augustus stepped back and watched Jason do what he came to do. From an inner jacket pocket he produced a vial, then snapped off several pieces of bark and shavings from the tree trunk, along with a handful of soil. Next Jason picked up the shovel and began digging, hauling away pile after pile until water bubbled through the surface.

Then he dug some more.

Unable to stand back any longer, Augustus joined the hunt, not knowing what he was searching for but wanting to be part of the process. Together the two men dug a hole the entire width between road and sidewalk, carving out the earth until the surface was above their heads. When the shovel was no longer useful Jason tossed it to the side and began using his hands. They were covered in mud and muck but still they dug, never speaking to each other, one focused on locating his treasure, the other merely helping him clear the path.

"There it is," Jason said reverently. Following his gaze, Augustus saw something sharp and grayish-white poking out from the bottom of their hole. It wasn't until the lab director had dug it out that he realized what it was—a bone. Human, most likely.

Augustus tried to back away, but hit the ground just one step behind him. Jason didn't notice, instead holding the bone fragment up to the moonlight with a sinister grin. All too soon he turned steely eyes to the tour guide.

"The greatest treasure of our time," he said, his voice rough and foreign and not belonging to a man at all. "Come, Augustus Jones. Let us complete our mission for this evening."

Together they climbed out of the hole and shoved the dirt back in place, packing it down with the shovel. It took the better part of an hour, and by the end they were sweaty, smeared with mud from head to toe, and brimming with eagerness.

From one side of the filled-in hole, Augustus watched Jason tuck the specimens in his pockets, a thought striking him the longer he observed the scene. "You already knew where this spot was. Why did you wait for me? You didn't need me to tell you where the victims were buried."

Smoothing down his jacket, Jason gave him the same knowing, ominous smirk. He lifted one hand to Augustus's face, his thumb stroking the man's cheek in a tender way. "No," he agreed softly, "but how could I accomplish such a feat and have no one to share it with?" Then he looked Augustus up and down. "Mr. Jones, you've made quite a mess of yourself. Perhaps you should hurry home and clean up."

Breathless, Augustus glanced down at his mud-covered shoes, his dirt-stained hands, and back up at Jason, stumbling back a step and gasping. He knew what his eyes saw, but his brain couldn't believe it. The man was clean. Spotless, even, nary a trace of mud or grass on him. Even his hair was dry beneath a crisp and clean hat.

"How...?" The question died on his tongue. It wasn't possible. It just wasn't possible for him to be filthy one second, then looking like he just stepped out of a magazine ad the next. But Jason only smiled and turned on his heel.

Augustus stared after him, and only when the other man had disappeared around the corner did his breath rush out of him, his body relaxing as though finally being released from an invisible force gripping his soul. All at once, the night came flooding back to him – this time with a different set of emotions. In place of curiosity, fear. Instead of want, disgust. And the final sensation, one of absolute terror.

What had they done?

CHAPTER 20

"You're thinking about it now, aren't you?"

Shaking his head to clear it, Augustus fought to focus on the matter at hand. That night in Savannah was long since passed and he hated to think of its consequences. The plague. Thousands dead. A bloodbath that spread through Jacksonville and into Savannah. And he'd been part of it.

Worse, he'd gotten pleasure out of it.

Pulling in a deep breath, Augustus looked up to find Jason staring at him. It was an even, deliberate stare, as though he knew exactly what was happening but waiting for Augustus to reach a conclusion on his own.

"I'm thinking about a lot of things," he answered. "Which would you like to discuss first? I'd love to know what you think of all the crazy shit going on lately."

"You're different," Jason commented, fingers drumming on the chair. "I remember *the* Augustus Jones, charismatic ghost tour guide who didn't believe in the stories he told every night, the amiable man who knew just how to charm the ladies. And now here you are, a frightened child in need of someone's hand to hold."

Indignation flared within Augustus. "This coming from the man who created a plague in order to cure it, and be the world's hero." He thought his comment would anger Jason, but the new hospital director was unaffected.

"What do you want, Augustus?"

"I want to know how you did it." He sat forward eagerly. "The Jason Waters I met the first time never would have done what you did. Something changed in you, something…. Something I couldn't explain then, and am only just now starting to understand. I've been running through that night in my head day after day after day. The way your voice sounded. What we did. The fact that one second you were covered in dirt and the next like you just got out of the shower." And the one thing he wouldn't voice—the way Jason made him feel, the seduction and lust that had swirled within him, blinded him.

Swallowing hard, Augustus finished with, "I want to know what happened to you, and if it's now happening to me."

"You went back in."

The reply surprised Augustus into a moment of silence. He sat back with a frown and tried to decipher its meaning. They hadn't gone anywhere the night Jason returned to Savannah, just to the cemetery to dig the hole and get his virus-contaminated specimens. "What?"

Jason lifted a shoulder in a bored shrug. "The house. You went back in."

"House? What house?"

The smirk Jason gave him was unamused. "*The* house, Augustus. The one you spend so much of your time talking about. The one you have now entered twice. The first time, you were lucky. You weren't ready yet, and so they couldn't latch on. But circumstances in your life changed over the past year, and so when you went in the second time, one of them was able to win the bid."

Augustus tried to make sense of a lecture that might as well have been gibberish. "The bid? What bid? Are you talking about the house on Abercorn?"

"That's how it works. You go into the house, see the flames, and they suck you in, until one of them wins the bid."

Augustus sighed at the seemingly circular conversation. "Who are *they*? What is the bid?"

"*They* are the ones lying in wait for unsuspecting fools like you and me to brave the hauntings and take a stroll through the house. The bid is the competition to win your soul."

"My soul?" he repeated incredulously. "Are you…are you trying to tell me that the house is filled with evil spirits, and that some, what, *demon* is bidding for my soul? And, what, that it happened to you too, the night we went in the house? Some demon won your soul and that's why you turned into some crazy plague-creating psychopath? Give me a break, Jason. This is completely—"

"Have you had the dreams?"

At the interruption, Augustus ran his hands down his face, through his hair. He didn't want to answer. Jason knew too much, and every question, every response, was bringing him that much closer to a truth he wasn't ready to hear.

"What…what dreams?"

"Augustus." Jason lifted a brow. "There's no use hiding these things from me."

The tone reminded Augustus of the way his father used to sound, so haughty, so condescending. "If you already know the answer, then stop asking stupid questions. Yes. I've had the dreams." His response was through clenched teeth.

"Then you understand what's happening and you know I speak the truth. The dreams are the bids. First you see the bids that lost. Then you dream the bid that won. Two minutes of our time to bid, entire hours in the netherworld, all to find the soul that calls to the demon. Once you accept the gift they offer, your entire world will change."

It was a physical and emotional pain when Augustus asked, "How?"

"Go back to the house if you really want to know. Enter the hallway of the floating flames. There is a spirit there, forced into an eternity as the keeper of angry spirits in punishment for straying from its given path. This spirit will answer all your questions."

"I'm never going back in that house." Augustus jumped to his feet. He couldn't sit here any longer and listen to such complete nonsense. Spirits haunting a house he'd stood in front of for more than ten years. A bid to win his soul. Dreams that tell the story of demons fighting to win him over to their side.

It was bullshit.

But...what if it wasn't? Augustus eyed Jason, or the man who looked like Jason Waters. He couldn't deny the man in front of him wasn't fully human. No regular, human man could have done what Jason did that night in Savannah, or develop a cure to a plague never before seen so fast, or rise to the top of the world as a virtual god in a man's body.

"It watches you, you know," Jason's voice cut into his thoughts. "From the window of the house, it watches you on your tours. It sees you leading so many people there, and wishes for someone to enter, just so it can finally be freed from its prison."

Before Augustus could say anything else, Jason rose as well and pressed a hand to the other man's shoulder. "You have two choices, Augustus. You can refuse the spirit and lose yourself, lie to yourself nothing is wrong until the demon has taken you over completely. Or you can embrace the gift you've been given, and witness just how powerful you can be.

"And, Augustus," Jason waited until the man had turned to face him, "I speak from experience. The power is phenomenal."

Augustus left the hospital torn between fearing for his mind and soul and looking forward to being the most empowered man in Georgia. If what Jason said was true—and he had no reason to lie—then he had a future filled with riches to look forward to.

He just wasn't sure what the cost would be.

At his car, Augustus moved to open the door, only to have a chunk of the handle break off in his fingers. "Are you fucking kidding me?" he asked no one in particular, fury welling within him at yet another thing damaged. He threw the piece of plastic in the grass and tipped his head back, needing a moment to collect his thoughts and calm down. In his pocket, he felt his cell phone buzz, but he ignored the call, unable to make conversation with the way his mind felt like it was fracturing apart.

Taking a moment to look up at the hospital, he imagined Jason watching him from his high-rise office with that calculated, perceptive leer. When his gaze lowered, it was to discover a handful of blue stones on the ground at his feet. Pure, beautiful, sparkling sapphires—an offering, he realized, to prove Jason's words.

He could take them, pocket the stones and sell them and keep every bit of the profit for himself. Or he could leave them, reject the notion of spirits after his soul who could give him everything he'd ever asked for.

The sapphires glittered against the asphalt, calling to him. "It's not real," he whispered, closing his eyes against the assault of blue sparkles, pretending everything in his life was perfectly normal. "You don't see a damn thing."

Except the smallest piece of the vast treasures coming to you.

"No," he tried to reject the voice in his head, that rough, garbled voice he now recognized as belonging to the Shax visitor in his dream. His breath tore out of his throat in a fearful gasp. "You're not real. There is no spirit. There is no bid. It's just a creepy house with a bad past."

Real is what you choose, Augustus Jones. What do you choose?

Despite the refusal on the tip of his tongue, Augustus found himself asking that question.

What did he choose? A home that fell apart every other day, a job where he was told what to do rather than making the rules, a bank account that never seemed to grow. Or did he choose wealth, a company he apparently created overnight and had everyone believing it was the next big thing, the ability to do whatever the hell he wanted.

"I want *my* life," he growled, but even as he spoke the words, he knew the truth hidden behind them. Yes, he wanted his life, but the life he deserved. The life he worked toward. *Not* the life his father had expected for him, a pathetic existence where he was worth nothing more than a pile of dog shit left to rot on the side of the road.

What life do you choose?

"I know what I want." Now his tone was firm, eyes unfocused as he zeroed in on the vision piecing itself together in his mind. A bright, wealth-filled future where his every need was provided for. And all he had to do was accept it.

No matter his choice, there would be a cost—a mediocre life with mediocre satisfaction but one that was entirely his, or accepting what Jason said was true and giving up his soul to a demon formerly trapped in a haunted house.

"How is any of this possible?" he whispered. And got an unsatisfying yet all-telling answer in return.

Make your choice, Augustus Jones.

*

It watched the moment Augustus made his decision. There was so much hesitation, doubt for one's sanity, but also hope for a brighter future. It knew how powerful hope could be—the most powerful of all emotions, more than fear, more than desperation. Hope for freedom was what kept the Will O'Wisp watching out the window every night. Hope for answers was what brought Jason Waters to the house a year ago.

And hope for an easier life would be the downfall of Augustus Jones.

Sadness mixed with relief filled the spirit when the man plucked the stones from the ground and dropped them into a waiting pocket. The Will O'Wisp could tell Augustus didn't fully believe in what was happening to him—perhaps he thought he was simply tired, or still dreaming, or maybe it was an act of defiance against the voice in his head—but what he believed no longer mattered.

Soon Augustus would realize the consequences of his choice. If he remembered the choice at all.

CHAPTER 21

He arrived home late that night, only belatedly realizing he had no idea if he had a tour scheduled, ultimately deciding he didn't care. If he really did have his own business, then he could do whatever he wanted, whenever he wanted to do it. Besides, he had a pocketful of sapphires that would earn him a hell of a lot more than an entire week's worth of tours.

Instead of worrying about work, he settled down on the couch and picked up the newspaper sitting on the coffee table. It was open to the crossword, which made him smile. Even now, his mother's favorite pastime remained the daily crossword, though she rarely was able to finish. Usually they completed them together, on nights they were able to eat dinner at the same time.

Tonight the crossword was almost complete, but as he looked over the answers, he realized many of them were simply letters filling in the blanks. It saddened him to see such blatant evidence of his mother's failing mental health.

But then something else caught his eye, a headline with his name in it. He recognized the byline as the woman who'd attempted to interview him earlier, one pushy and arrogant Rebecca Wright, and the picture next to the article was one from the ghost tour company's website, rather than the surprised snapshot when he'd opened the door. He'd forgotten the reporter was a freelance journalist, her name appearing in the paper as often as her face appeared on the television screen. And while he hadn't watched his news interview, he was interested in what the papers were saying.

Savannah's Favorite Ghost Tour Guide Goes National, the headline read.

"Oh, really," he mumbled, skimming the article to find a lot of information about himself he'd never known before. Him, Augustus Jones, buying out his former ghost tour company and renaming it, keeping on the same team that apparently was oh-so-supportive and excited to be part of his company, and already in the works to expand his tour offerings to other cities, which were yet to be revealed.

"Because I have no fucking clue what's happening," he said, racking his brain for memories of this new development and coming up blank.

The television flickered to life, startling Augustus into dropping the paper. He was about to grab the remote when he saw what, or rather, *who*, was on the screen—himself. Immediately engrossed, Augustus turned up the volume and watched what was an entire documentary of his life.

Except, not as he remembered it.

His childhood was the same. An abusive father who drank too much and hit too often, a mother who cowered beneath his fist until the day he walked out of their tiny Denver trailer and never came back. Gert finding the strength she'd lost and moving across the country with her young son, finding a new home in Savannah. A scrawny, shy Augustus exploring a city of ghost stories, falling in love with the soul of the town, the life pulsing around it. A little boy growing up with lofty dreams of being a rich and famous actor, but never knowing where to start, finding a foot in the door as a ghost tour guide for Sonny Harvest.

Then his life took a detour from the known and remembered. Augustus sat forward, brow furrowed as he watched himself become Sonny's assistant, first going out on tours and building a name for himself as a local favorite. But he was more than just a guide, he saw with interest. He was being groomed to take over. Then came the day of Tessa Taylor's tour, one Augustus remembered well, and the aftermath.

Reporters hounded Augustus, wanting to know more about Tessa. He gave interviews, offered insight for a TV movie, and, he saw with interest, he wrote that book he was offered. Breaking his attention from the TV for only a moment, Augustus looked over at the bookshelf, lips parting in a surprised smile at the novel with his name etched down the spine.

He was known nationwide, paid handsomely for his interviews, and then Jason Waters became the hero who saved everyone from the RYF-2 epidemic. Again more people wanted to know who Jason was and flocked to Augustus, the Savannah savant.

His local fame boosted their business and day and night tours alike were booked solid. Augustus, Mel, Voodoo, and Silas never had an empty tour, and all four were paid well for their exciting walks around town. Mel hung on his arm, lips frequently pressed to his, all those dates he'd once been denied forgotten. And then came the day Sonny handed the business over.

"Now we're getting somewhere," Augustus whispered. His hands rubbed together in excitement.

Sonny was ready to retire, and, with no children of his own, gave the business to Augustus, who promptly renamed it and began constructing plans to expand. And now here he was, business owner.

What happened next was apparently up to him.

A new life is just the beginning of what I can grant you, came the voice in his head. *A token of faith.*

Before Augustus could even think about what that meant, let alone reply, the screen changed, signaling the end of his new lifetime in review. But the scene before him now was far more interesting anyway. Rebecca Wright was delivering the eleven o'clock news. She wore a tight pink dress that accented all her curves, hair in soft waves around her face, but that was where the gentleness stopped.

"Police chased the suspect down River Street," she was saying into the camera while gesturing to the river behind her. "They caught him here, knocking him flat on his ass and making the arrest."

Augustus snorted at her language, and at the surprised expression on the anchorman's face on the other side of the split screen. But Rebecca wasn't finished.

"Residents of Savannah can rest easy and feel safe again in their homes knowing this piece of shit is off the streets and behind bars. I'm sure we can all agree our fine city is better off without these mother fu—"

The split screen cut off, removing Rebecca from view and showing only the anchorman, who tried to recover from the on-air cursing with a nervous smile. "Thank you, Rebecca," he said smoothly and transitioned into the rest of the news.

"What a shame."

Augustus glanced over his shoulder to see Gert standing in the living room doorway, a frown crossing her face. "What is?"

"That lovely young woman. She was such a good reporter, with such a bright future. Now she's gone and ruined her career with that foul language."

Augustus frowned as his mother sat next to him. All amusement left him. Considering her words, he realized she was right. The reporter would be fined, possibly fired, for those few slips, and for what? Because he abused his power and essentially told her to curse on air, all because of a surprise interview?

Guilt started to seep in, but before he could dwell on it, his mother asked, "Have you seen my crossword, Augustus?"

"Yes, it's right...." He trailed off in the middle of retrieving the paper, slowly turning back to Gert. "What did you just call me?"

She looked at her son like he'd just lost his mind. "Augustus, of course. That is your name."

"What…what about Nathaniel?"

Now she *really* looked at him like he was nuts, he noted. "Who is Nathaniel?"

For a long moment, Augustus stared at his mom, surprised by how sad it made him to hear her reply. For so many years, all he'd wanted was to hear her say those words, to call him Augustus Jones and know him as that persona. Now that it was actually happening, it broke his heart.

She forgot him. His own mother's memories had been changed, because of a lie that slipped out on accident.

"Augustus? Is that my crossword?" Not noticing the dilemma in his eyes, Gert pointed at the paper on the floor.

Blinking a few times to snap out of the daze, Augustus nodded and retrieved the paper. "Yeah, Mom. Here it is." His voice was thick and he needed to get out of there before tears fell. Annoying, unwelcomed, pathetic tears. He rose quickly and kissed the top of her head. "I'm gonna hit the hay, Mom. See you in the morning."

Rushing to his room, Augustus closed the door behind him and pressed his forehead against it. Too many thoughts raced through his mind, thoughts mixed with feelings of guilt, fear, and disturbing excitement. He'd lied to so many people, and now he was seeing the consequences—people's lives being ruined all because of him.

With a sigh, Augustus shrugged out of his jacket and shirt, then stepped out of his pants. A thunk against the floor reminded him he'd missed a call after leaving the hospital. He retrieved the phone from his pant pocket and scrolled to his missed calls, not recognizing the number.

Seconds after dialing his voicemail, Shelby Cross's stern and all-business voice spoke in his ear, "Hello, Mr. Jones, this is Shelby Cross from Smithfield Bank. I'm calling to discuss your account discrepancy that we reviewed a couple days ago, in regards to missing funds out of your savings account. I've been reviewing the information and would like to talk to you further about this and see if we can come to an understanding. Please call me back directly."

The rest of her message faded away as Augustus deciphered the real meaning to the phone call. Her tone, the careful wording, the request to call her back directly, all pointed to one thing—she suspected something was wrong.

"That wasn't supposed to happen." He meant for the complaint to be sent inward, but instead it just made him sound like a petulant child. Now on top of worrying about his mother and his apparent new business, he had to figure out what to do about Shelby and the, if he was being completely honest, stolen money.

Have faith, said the voice in his head. *Tomorrow brings with it new treasures for a new life.*

"Yeah, right," Augustus muttered, but didn't push the matter. He simply chose to hope for the best, and readied himself for bed.

CHAPTER 22

The team was waiting for him when Augustus went to work the next day, gathered around the ticket shack and holding their schedules. The booth looked different, freshly painted a solid black rather than a peeling yellow, and outlined in white lights glowing even in broad daylight. A sign hung from the counter that boasted the new company name, along with a picture of Augustus looking just the right mix of charming and devilish.

"Boss man," Voodoo greeted with a brow lifted, as excited as his face ever looked. Silas merely offered a nod as he read over his tours for the week. Mel, though, watched him curiously as he checked for his own schedule, only to realize he didn't have one.

"Work is for the little people," she said, but there was an air of humor to her tone that had him smiling—a smile that dropped in surprise when she lifted herself up to her toes and planted a kiss to his mouth. "You were supposed to call me last night. What happened?"

Still tasting her lips long after she pulled them away, Augustus couldn't help but slide an arm around her back, tugging her closer like he'd always wanted to do. "Sorry, babe. Got caught up taking care of Mom." Then, because he knew he could, he stole another kiss from her, lingering against her mouth for a few blissful seconds. Her hands curled in his shirt, but when he pulled away, Mel's grin had disappeared. In its place was uncertainty, and the sudden change in attitude concerned him.

Silas's voice cut into the moment. "So, we read the paper. First you change our name, now you're planning to expand? When were you going to tell us this?"

"Uh...just working out some details first." He had no idea how to cover for a decision he technically didn't even remember. His eyes never left Mel's as she spoke. "Everything okay?" he asked so only she could hear.

"Yeah," she answered, but it was an unsure reply and they both knew it. "I just need a moment." Without waiting for a response, Mel turned on her heel and headed away from the booth. All three of the men watched her leave, the guides offering Augustus dismissive shrugs before grabbing their schedules and going their separate ways. After a moment he followed, her rapid retreat leading him away from the ticket shack to a bench along the river. He was silent the entire time, only speaking after they had both taken a seat.

"What's up, Mel? You just went from happy to almost scared in about a second flat."

Mel stared out at the river, her blue eyes narrowed in concentration. "I'm not sure. I was so happy to see you when you got here, then when you kissed me, it was like my head just started spinning."

He grinned over at her and was appalled by his own reaction, though it couldn't stop him from replying, "Well, I do have that effect on the ladies."

"Augustus," Mel sighed. "I'm being serious." Waiting until he sobered, wiping the smirk from his face, she continued, "I don't mean spinning in that, totally in love, lost in the feel of another person kind of way. That's what we had when we first started dating, remember?"

He didn't, and it angered him that he'd missed what could have been such an amazing memory. *So you give me a great life but I can't remember any of it*, he grumbled internally, belatedly realizing the complaint only further proved how much he actually believed what Jason told him.

"Anyway, this spinning is like…like whenever I see you lately, my body feels like it's being pulled in two different directions. One part of me wants to be with you. The other part feels like it wants to run away." She looked down at her hands and sighed again, the sound saddening him. "I don't know. Maybe I just need a few days off after this week or something. I've been feeling weird the past few days anyway so hopefully I'm just coming down with something."

He frowned over at her, seeing the concern in her expression, the worry for her own health. And it made him feel like an asshole that he was the cause of it all. Still, he didn't know how to help. "Mel…do you remember the conversation we had the other day?"

"The other day? When I came to see you after your mom fell?" He nodded and she leaned forward, elbows on her knees. "Sure. I remember when you asked me what I believed about Savannah. Ghosts and spirits and stuff."

"Right. And do you remember running out on me?"

"Running out?" Her faced turned up to his, so young and innocent, so confused. "I didn't run out. I spent the night. Except…." As though her mind finally caught up, Mel sucked in a deep, gasping breath. "Except I remember you telling me all these things about how people believe whatever you say. And I feel like it scared me, but if it did, why did I stay?"

There was only one answer he could give to soothe her frazzled nerves, and it was the one answer he could never speak. Even now, watching the turmoil Mel faced, Augustus couldn't tell her the truth, couldn't risk having it all taken away. Not if it was real, and he was actually living this new life. If it was a dream, well, then soon he would wake up and all would be back to normal.

This is your new normal, Augustus Jones.

He almost welcomed the return of the stork-beast's voice. *Why is Mel so confused?*

Some are resistant to the ways of the darkness. Some see through the veil. They are the dangerous ones. The ones who risk you losing it all.

Mel was somehow immune to his lies, Augustus mused, and yet, not quite. He was thinking about the consequences of that fact when she began speaking again.

"I feel…I feel like my mind can't catch up to reality, you know? Like I remember you always trying to go out with me and me always rejecting you, but now I feel like all I want to do is be with you. Why did my feelings change so suddenly? And we'd always been colleagues in this company, and now all of a sudden you're my boss and even though I *know* that was always the plan, because I can see those memories in my head, it still feels weird, like my brain can't accept it."

Her fear and pain tugged on his heart. "What can I do to make it better, Mel?"

"I don't know." She shrugged, defeated. "Tell me I'm not crazy. Tell me this life, you taking over the business, us dating, tell me it's not what we've been living all along. Tell me I'm right."

Tell her she's wrong.

The command nearly forced him to do just that. Augustus caught himself before he spoke. He couldn't break her like that. Not Mel. *His* Mel. He couldn't let her hurt, which meant he had to confess. Maybe she would believe him, maybe not. Either way his conscious would be cleared.

"Mel, the reason you're feeling and thinking these things is because I'm not—"

The word *myself* stuck in his throat, a physical barrier blocking air and tightening the muscles in his neck. Augustus paused, relaxing his mind and body, then cleared his throat and tried again. "I went—"

The unfinished *"into the house on Abercorn"* lodged in his throat. He gasped for air, Mel striking him on the back in a meek attempt to help. But nothing could help him, he now understood, because he couldn't speak the truth. He would never be able to tell her she was right if he couldn't get the words out.

You chose this, Augustus Jones. Now you must live the life you chose.

Regret battled with acceptance as the Shax's voice echoed in his head. Augustus rubbed at his throat. "Sorry," he rasped out. "Swallowed wrong."

"And, see? The way your voice sounded just then. I *know* that's not what your voice sounds like. But I also remember hearing it from the first day we met. You're different, Augustus. I just don't know how."

Though he hated to say it, he replied, "Maybe you're different, Mel."

"Maybe *you* are," she challenged. "Don't put this on me when you're sounding creepy and buying out businesses all of a sudden. I *know* something is going on with you and it's somehow affecting me. I just don't know what it is."

"Do the others feel the same way?"

Her eyes narrowed, though they still glinted with the slightest hint of crazed panic. "Not that I've noticed. But you know Voodoo and Silas. They are just here for the paycheck and do whatever you ask."

"That's all I can expect of my guides." Forcing himself back into the persona of Augustus Jones, businessman, he didn't let himself react to her words. "Take as much time as you need, Mel. I...I guess I don't really know what to tell you. This was always the plan, for me to take over. As for you and me...I guess I'll leave that up to you as far as what you want to do about it."

He needed to get away from her, before he said something to reveal just how right she was to be confused—assuming he could voice the confession, anyway. With a gentle pat on her shoulder, he rose and walked away, willing himself not to look back.

CHAPTER 23

Mel couldn't accept her new world, her mind caught between realities. Augustus couldn't explain how the world had changed overnight, how some creature called the Shax altered reality for possibly every person on earth—or at least those who'd ever known Augustus—but he also wasn't going to try.

For once in his life, he was going to go with the flow and hope everything would work out in his favor. No more busting his ass day in and day out to make a buck. Just enjoying the ride...even if that ride took him to the nearest psych ward because he was seeing nonexistent storks and stealing money from banks and thinking everyone believed his made-up stories.

Not wanting to deal with people, Augustus locked himself away in the storage unit that now belonged to him, organizing the dozens of costumes and muttering beneath his breath. With each box he moved, every rack he shoved out of the way, his anger grew until he was stewing in the knowledge that someone dared to doubt him, even if it was the woman he lusted over.

"I'm Augustus fucking Jones," he said through his teeth. "I don't have to take shit from anyone."

Only when midnight had fallen did he leave the unit. He didn't remember how long he'd worked or if he'd eaten, only felt the searing fury that even in his new life, someone was giving him shit he didn't deserve.

He wasn't going to take it anymore.

His stomp-filled stroll took him to Colonial Park Cemetery. Contrary to the stories told during tours, he loved the cemetery, its peaceful atmosphere, and found it a relaxing rather than haunted place. He could spend hours looking through the bars at the old tombstones, imagining how life must have been back then. So much easier, he liked to believe. During the day, he'd often sit at one of the benches placed throughout beneath an oak tree, basking in the sunny quiet. He hoped it would bring him peace now, so he didn't go home and face his mother while feeling such discontentment.

The sound of hushed mumblings reached his ears as he walked by the cemetery tonight, far after midnight with few people left out on tours and bar hops. Augustus frowned and paused by the back entrance to the cemetery, noting the lock on the gate had been picked open and was slightly ajar.

Annoyed that some idiot tourists were likely holed up next to a grave trying to see spirits, Augustus entered the cemetery, following the sound of voices until he reached the back wall, which was lined with old headstones. There weren't many places to hide in the cemetery, but the small group tucked against the wall was doing a decent job, having situated themselves between the headstones and a cluster of shrubs.

There were four people total, three boys and one girl, all appearing to be late teenagers. They huddled around a pentagram roughly cut into the grass and had small candles burning at each of the star's points. Two were holding hands and mumbling something, the other two looking on with excited fear shining in their eyes.

For a moment, Augustus stood back in the shadows and watched, hands in the pockets of his long black cloak, face mostly concealed by the collar. It wasn't the first time he'd caught some stupid kids doing stupid things in the cemetery, thinking it was fun to try to conjure up spirits they knew nothing about. Usually he just kept walking, but sometimes it was fun to give them exactly what they were looking for.

Let us show these children what evil truly looks like.

Augustus understood the voice in his head now, welcomed it even. "How will we do that?" he asked quietly, eyes trained on the teenagers. They were still chanting, heads tipped up to the night sky, faces lit in the soft glow of tea-light candles.

You need only search your soul for the true Augustus Jones.

The true Augustus Jones. He wanted that, ached for it. And so he closed his eyes and took in a deep breath, feeling the air fill him, travel through his body, rejuvenate him. He felt his heartbeat slow, his blood warm, and when he opened his eyes, he saw the world through a new kind of lens. Everything was brighter, clearly outlined with the smallest of details defined in tree trunks and flower petals and individual blades of grass, all of it more inviting than ever before.

Mine for the taking.

With his newfound confidence and sight, Augustus stepped forward, his boots snapping twigs in the grass. The teenagers jumped at the sound, spinning around and peering through the starlight at their visitor, seeing only a shadowed figure standing statue-still, arms clasped behind his back, with a thick coat billowing out behind him in a sudden cold breeze. The girls gasped and stumbled back behind their boyfriends, one of whom plucked a knife from the grass and held it cautiously at his side.

"Who are you?" the one with the knife demanded. He was a fit and clean-cut-looking boy, perhaps a member of a local fraternity house.

"What do you want?" the other one asked when no response was given. He was equally fit, though the tattoo on the side of his neck suggested he was less than proper.

Augustus looked at them both in turn, then moved his eyes to the girls. It was clear which one belonged to each boy—the pretty blonde in designer clothes and the leather-jacket-wearing biker chick. How these duos came together, he would never know, because they wouldn't get the chance to answer.

"Who the fuck are you, man?" the first one asked again, and this time Augustus answered.

"I am the commander of the thirty legions," he boasted, head held high. "I am the Great Marquis of Hell, he who holds power over the thirty demon legions."

The tattooed teen laughed, sparing his friends an incredulous smirk. "Yeah, okay, pal. Look, how about I give you a few bucks and point you to the closest shelter, and you let us get back to—"

"Back to what?" Augustus interrupted, stepping closer. "Were you not calling to the darkness? Seeking the spirits of the dead?" A smile slowly crossed his face at their silence. He could almost smell the fear radiating off the girls, the same fear so obvious in their wide eyes.

But only the girls were the smart ones, for they knew to be afraid. The frat boy stood and pointed at Augustus. "This isn't funny, man. It's time for you to go."

"Go? Do you not want to finish your ritual? My friends were just coming to meet you." Even Augustus wasn't sure where that statement came from. But just as he wondered, the answer came to him in a flash behind his eyes, a memory from a long, long time ago.

Oh, how powerful I could be.

"What-what friends?" one of the girls stammered, her hands clutching her boyfriend's arm. In the star and candlelight, her frightened face nearly made Augustus shiver in anticipation. But he held still, breathing in deeply and tipping his head back as though summoning the spirits called forth by the ritual.

In that moment, crickets ceased to chirp. Rustling leaves stilled. The air thinned, threatening to steal the breaths of four foolish teenagers with one ill-advised idea. They huddled together, feet scraping atop their crudely made pentagram, but before they could attempt to flee, the earth began to rumble.

Trees shook from roots to canopy. The ground split, the resounding crack echoing throughout the cemetery in tune with the cavern that formed a circle around the five. Dirt was spit up from the gaping void, pieces of earth flying upwards and spinning in a nonexistent wind, round and round the ones who called to the darkness.

Through it all Augustus never moved, his smirk ever present and stare trained on the teenagers. Not until the swirling earth stopped did he shift from his statuesque stance. He looked over both shoulders slowly, pleased to see the legion of ghouls on horseback on either side of him. Thirty black horses stomped at the ground impatiently, saliva dripping from open mouths, large and dark eyes seeing all. Atop their backs sat the soldiers of Hell, hands gripping frayed leather reigns, awaiting orders from their commander.

The leather-clad girl reacted first, attempting to flee her friends. She rushed away from the remaining trio, only to stumble backward and fall when one of the riders pushed forward, threatening to knock her down. The soldiers all advanced then, keeping the four trapped within a tight circle.

"Please." One boy held up a hand—a shaking hand, Augustus noted with sick glee. "We don't want any trouble. We just wanted to have some fun. We never thought anything was actually going to happen."

"No," Augustus purred, "but something happened nonetheless. The question is, what are you going to do about it?" He stepped forward, finally coming into view.

"Hey." The blonde teenager pointed at him. "I-I know you. You're that tour guide guy. But," she looked around and swallowed hard before continuing, "I-I-I don't understand how you did this.

What's going on? You're just a guy. You're not supposed to be able to...."

When she stopped speaking, her friends turned to look, not understanding why she was clutching at her throat, mouth opening and closing. The girl screamed but no sound escaped. The silence made her scream harder, her face reddening with the strain, muscles cording in her throat.

"You son of a bitch!" her boyfriend yelled, leaping into action—only to stumble over his own feet and fall to the ground. He blinked and wiped at his eyes, gasped and clawed at the grass, unable to form words in his blindness.

All the while Augustus watched with his head cocked, fascinated by his newfound power. *I give you the gift to take away sight, hearing, and voice*, spoke the Shax in his mind. *A most powerful and useful gift.*

"When you are careless with your actions, you suffer the consequences," Augustus spoke calmly to the remaining two, who were smart enough not to reply or even move. Nor did they try to help their friends. "When you make foolish decisions, you call upon forces beyond your ability to understand."

"We're sorry," the not-so-tough chick in her expensive leather jacket whispered. "We really didn't mean anything by it. We just... we just want to go home."

Augustus offered the girl his signature charming smile. "Home?" he repeated, his voice low and seductive. "My legion is here to bring you home."

He waited for the weight of his words to sink in, all the while basking in their fear and observing them each in turn. The boy with the neck tattoo, one arm in front of his girlfriend in a noble yet ineffective attempt to protect her. The girl in the leather jacket, pretty brown eyes filled with tears and heart pounding so hard he could hear its vibrations in the air. Next to her sat the speechless teenager, one hand holding her throat, the other gripping her boyfriend's shoulder, keeping him in place as he desperately tried to feel his way to freedom.

When the four were still, understanding the only way out of the cemetery was at the mercy of the man who stood before them, Augustus closed the distance. He kneeled to their level, only now showing his hands, which were each gripping sharp, four-inch-long curved blades. Where they came from, he didn't know, but he didn't care.

"Please, don't," the sighted boy said with a quiver to his voice.

Augustus lifted a brow. "You forget, foolish children. Every call to the darkness requires its sacrifice."

The boy swallowed hard and nodded once. "Let the others go. I'll…I'll take their place."

"A noble sacrifice," Augustus replied to the sound of the girl's hushed refusal. "But not nearly enough."

Take them, the Shax demanded, allowing one momentary glimpse of clarity. *Take them, and with their deaths, the ritual will be complete.*

To the legion Augustus ordered, "Cleanse the city of the confused and non-believers." To the cluster of petrified cemetery visitors he added, "I will take care of the rest."

CHAPTER 24

Dawn was breaking through the horizon when Augustus returned home, the beautiful golden sky hiding the horrors it had seen just a few short hours before. When he stepped through the front door, his hands were clean, his clothes pristine, and his face lit with a satisfied smile.

He could still smell their blood, could still hear their screams—until he silenced them all with a simple flick of his wrist. How they crawled around the cold earth, clutching their throats, begging for someone, anyone, to hear their pleas for help.

And how it felt, such unbridled power coursing through him, guiding his hand as it lowered the blade through flesh. So smooth and easy, so peaceful, with only the sound of impatient stallions occasionally stomping at the earth. Not even the tears mixing with hot blood or desperate hands clawing for escape could have dampened his mood.

"Good morning, son."

Brought out of his recollections of last night, Augustus lowered his hand, unaware he'd even been observing it. "Good morning," he replied evenly, no trace of sinister delight evident in his tone. "I'm sorry I'm late. New business and all."

Gert patted him on the cheek. "My son, successful businessman. I'm so proud of you." Then she took him by the hand and began pulling him toward the kitchen. "You work too hard and deserve a hot, home-cooked meal every morning, just as I've always done for my little boy. Let me make you breakfast before you have to get back to work," Gert insisted, moving her son to a bar stool. "You work too hard."

He didn't tell her she'd just said that, knowing her fragile mind couldn't always remember thoughts passing through each second. Instead Augustus watched with dark eyes as his mother moved to the fridge and pulled out a carton of eggs and slab of bacon, then retrieved a pan. Some part of him felt this was wrong, letting such an old and frail woman slave over a hot stove, but another part was tired of being the one to always take care of things.

A man of power is pampered, came the raucous voice in his head. *He does not do the pampering.*

So he continued to watch, his carefully relaxed expression crumbling into a frown only when his mother went to turn on the second burner and the knob popped off in her arthritic hand. At that he moved, sliding off the stool and rounding the counter, taking the knob from her. Only five months ago he'd had an appliance specialist come out to repair one of the burners. Now a different one was literally falling apart.

"This won't do," he murmured. Fingers tightening around the knob, he looked around at the faded and peeling paint, down at the worn laminate floors, the décor that had certainly seen better days. It was disgusting, all of it. Disgusting and disappointed and embarrassing.

"This is not a home fit for us."

"It's our home," Gert replied, too distracted by the stove and her need to cook a big breakfast to notice the glimmer in his eyes. "And I love it because we are together, and we are happy."

Augustus peered down at her, taking her by the arms. "We can be happier in luxury."

"Where are you going?" From the stove, Gert crossed her arms and gave a pointed look at the egg carton. "I have three other burners to cook breakfast with."

"Later, Mother," Augustus promised. "We will have a wonderful breakfast, an even better dinner, and many more meals like we've never experienced before. I will fix this for us both. I will give myself the life I have worked hard for, and so too shall you reap the benefits of caring for your son."

He left her standing in the kitchen, baffled by his strange speech, odd wording, and the way his voice transformed into something she didn't recognize.

*

He chose to walk, taking his time to saunter along sleepy sidewalks beneath expansive oak trees allowing for bright morning sunlight to filter between green leaves. The city was starting to come to life the closer he got downtown, and Augustus watched it all through fresh eyes, seeing Savannah for everything it had to offer him.

No longer was he just another cog working in the system. A faceless, disposable worker bee breaking his back for the queen. "Now, *I* am king," he said to himself, pride puffing out his chest.

Everywhere he looked he saw opportunity for his takeover. New streets to lead tour groups on. An empty building for lease that could serve as headquarters and maybe even a gift shop for Beware!

Imagine the possibilities, Augustus Jones.

A tremor working its way through his foot had Augustus pausing mid-step. He glanced around, not seeing any signs of a quake other than the strange tugging sensation within his body. It led his feet of its own accord, drawing a path in his mind's eye. Down Abercorn, just past East Wayne on the other side of the old Espy house, to the center of Calhoun Square.

The tremor strengthened the closer he walked to the square, all but vibrating his entire body by the time he came to a stop.

Something was here, beckoning to him, and he obliged the vision granted to him by fate or demon or whatever else it might have been. Kneeling, Augustus dug down a few inches, feeling a humming in the earth that directed him to the right, down another few inches. Soon his fingers touched what he guessed was a stone. He made quick work of unburying it, tugging the piece free from the soil and holding it up to the light.

Not a stone, he saw with reverence, but gold. A chunk of gold the size of his palm.

"Beautiful," he murmured, wiping away the dirt and polishing the gold on his shirt until it sparkled. "But where did you come from?"

Calhoun Square was frequently traveled, gardened, played upon by children. There was no possible way a piece of gold this size could have stayed hidden. "So how did you get there now?"

It was a question he asked himself as well as directed internally, hoping for guidance and receiving none. Pocketing the small treasure with a shrug, Augustus resumed his walk, which took him close to Colonial Park Cemetery. As he approached, he saw blue lights flashing across the tombstones. A few more steps brought police cars into view, nearly hidden behind the wall of spectators craning their necks, trying to get a view of the grisly scene roped off in the back of the cemetery.

Augustus stopped at the back of the crowd, hands in his jacket pockets to ward off the chill. Even from here he could hear whispers floating throughout the crowd. Some speculations, some repetitions of police orders, some proudly stating what they managed to see from the gates.

One of those spectators caught sight of him and pointed. "Hey! You're Augustus Jones, the ghost tour guy! We signed up for one of your company's tours for tomorrow night!"

Augustus nodded down at the woman, whom he guessed was a tourist based on the camera hanging from her neck. In his most charming Irish accent he replied, "I appreciate the business, ma'am."

"Will your guides be taking us by this cemetery? Will they tell us what's going on in there?"

"The guides all tell their own stories," he answered breezily. "As I don't know what's going on in there just yet, I can't say if they will mention it."

"I'll tell you what's going on." This came from a man who was pushing his way through the crowd, back toward the sidewalk. "I saw it just before the cops came and pushed us all back. Four kids murdered. Mid-to-late teens, they said. Police said it looks like some kinda cult ritual."

The woman shivered, wrapping her coat tighter around herself. "They committed suicide?"

"Nah." The man shook his head. "I heard one cop on the radio, said it looked like their hearts had been cut out of their bodies."

"Their *hearts*?" another busybody repeated. "Why would someone do such a thing?"

"Take their heart, take their power." All eyes turned to Augustus, but he was peering through the crowd toward the cemetery, breathing in the scent of soil, sweat, and lingering blood. Before long his gaze landed on a stork, *his* stork, perched on the roof of a police car.

The others must have followed his gaze, because he heard murmurs of, "Look at that bird…. Staring at the cemetery…. Must see something…. Now it's looking at us…. Why isn't the noise scaring it away?"

Augustus hid a smile at their musings. He knew the stork's presence was a reminder of what he'd done—what he'd gotten away with. *Take their heart, take their power.* He hadn't felt so young, so full of energy and life and ideas, in a long time. It was just a refreshing sensation that he couldn't find it within himself to care about the carnage he'd caused.

"Cops said they are looking for someone on horseback." The comment interested Augustus. He peered over at the man who had shared details earlier. "Yeah, I heard them saying the ground was packed down, like a herd of horses passed through sometime in the middle of the night. They can't explain it, and Savannah is full of horses, so they are looking for a needle in a haystack right now."

At the horrified look on the camera-wielding woman's face, Augustus tipped his head down and whispered, "Enjoy your ghost tour, ma'am," then resumed his stroll, wanting to get away from further speculation of what happened last night.

CHAPTER 25

A half-hour later he reached his destination—a stunning two-story brick home with Colonial flair mixed with Southern hospitality. The house sat on five acres, with well-manicured beds filled with colorful plants he didn't know the name of, and hundred-year-old oaks reaching for the clear blue sky, Spanish moss draped from their limbs. It was peaceful, beautiful, though his lust for the house was never about the yard, but about the home itself.

Majestic was a word he'd often thought of to describe the house. Perfectly symmetrical gray bricks accented white-trim windows, a high V-peaked two-tier roof, and an expansive white-wood porch that wrapped the entire front and south side. A three-car carport stretched out from the north face, opening up to a wide paver driveway lined in flowering shrubs. Far behind the house, surrounded by oak trees, was a tennis court, and next to it a gorgeous infinity pool with a built-in bar that was rarely used but always in pristine condition.

Bypassing the stone pathway leading through a vine-covered archway, Augustus headed for the front door.

His casual gait never lessened as Augustus approached the house, stopping at the wide and slate-gray front door. He took a moment to peer up at the etched glass windows stretching from floor to ceiling, the ornate lights lining the length of the porch, before reaching for the doorknob. It didn't surprise him to find the door open easily for him. He entered, calm and confident, passing through a foyer of built-in bookcases lining the entire wall down to what he knew would eventually open up into an expansive living room with bay windows overlooking the backyard gardens.

Pine floors stretched from wall to wall, leading into a den to his left with a marble wood-burning fireplace. But he didn't stop to admire the rooms. Augustus followed the sounds of clinking dishes, his steps light on the wood floors, hands in his pockets as he entered the kitchen. Though he'd only been in the room twice, it had never been hard to imagine himself there, cooking his mother breakfast on the glass-top stove, keeping their food cold in the most upgraded stainless steel refrigerator, or stocked in the walk-in pantry. He loved this kitchen, with its gray tiles and white cabinets, wide windows letting in plenty of natural sunlight.

"Augustus? What are you doing in here?" Sonny asked from the breakfast table, shocked into putting down his fork. Across from him, his wife, Barb, appeared equal parts curious and annoyed.

"What do you mean?" Augustus asked smoothly, his voice low and gravelly. "This is my home."

The look shared between husband and wife was comical to Augustus, but his expression remained stoic, hands clasped behind his back. Sonny rose from the table. "Excuse me? Is this some kind of joke? Because I don't get it. What are you doing in here?"

"This is my home," Augustus repeated. The next words came to him as though by magic. "As part of our business agreement, any and all property belonging to Harvest Haunts, formerly owned by Sonny Harvest, is transferred to me, Augustus Jones, to conclude our transaction. As I have purchased your company, so too did I purchase your home, which is listed, for tax and business purposes, as the headquarters for Harvest Haunts. As such, it is the headquarters for the company I purchased and renamed."

The lie flowed easily from his lips. It wasn't one he'd even thought of on the walk over; he'd simply planned to walk in and say this was his home. But the demon within had given him a cover, and a believable one at that.

Sonny looked torn between believing the lie and wanting to argue. He'd stood up and tossed his napkin to the table, crossing his arms. Augustus could only assume the lie hadn't yet taken hold in his former boss's mind. "This has been my home for twenty years."

"And now it will be mine for another twenty, as you finally leave the town that has held you back from your full potential." What that potential was, Augustus would leave Sonny to discover. He knew his old boss had money saved up from previous careers and from his successful business, just as everyone in Savannah knew his pretty little trophy wife came from one of the wealthiest families in the state. Surely they would find somewhere new to live that met their standards.

Augustus approached them, running his fingertips across the top of the glass table. "Perhaps you and your lovely wife remember sitting at this very table, discussing the ins and outs of the business sale. It was during this conversation where you and Barb mentioned how excited you were to just pick up and move to California, where you've always dreamed of living, leaving this boring and stifling city behind in favor of life filled with sunshine and beaches. How exciting it was to no longer be tied down by a business that worked you day and night, to finally be free to do whatever you wanted in the state you've always known was where you were meant to be."

As he spoke, he saw the nonexistent meeting in his mind, the three of them pouring over a stack of papers and carefully signing each one while two men he assumed were attorneys watched over the transaction. He watched himself sometime in the recent past, dressed in a suave suit and wearing an expression he'd never before seen on his face, suspiciously cold and void of the charm that made him, him.

And he saw, right now in this sunny kitchen, the moment the false memory was implanted in Sonny and Barb's heads as well. They looked at one another for a long minute, smiles growing on their faces as they remembered conversations that never happened at all. Augustus took a step back and let them piece it all together.

"We wanted to be on the road by this weekend," Barb said with a dreamy expression, perhaps picturing their new life across the country. Her brow was creased, and Augustus knew it was because her mind was fighting to connect the dots while envisioning a new life never meant for her at all. "Honey, did you remember to book our flights? We wanted a morning flight, first class, of course."

"We're driving, remember? A nice, long road trip before we settle in a new place," Sonny replied.

Interesting, Augustus thought, eyes narrowed as he listened to their conversation. His lie created a shared dream between them, but with some of the smaller details changed.

"I...I don't remember a road trip being part of the plan." Now her voice had an edge to it. "That is a very long drive, Sonny."

"But so beautiful. And it will give us a chance to reconnect." Sonny smiled over at his wife, then pressed a kiss to her cheek when she, too, offered a grin.

"I guess you're right. That could be fun, and we're not in any hurry. We have plenty of time to ease into our new life." Then her eyes widened and she looked around frantically. "But we need to pack our clothes! And figure out movers to bring the things we want to keep! There is so much to do."

Before the two could work themselves into a tizzy, Augustus cut in, "Feel free to take your time with your things. Get out to California, find a new home you love, then worry about getting your things there. It will just be me, and my mother, and our limited belongings. There is no rush for either of you."

Barb clapped her hands together once, all traces of concern gone. "I'm going to start packing for the road. Come on, Sonny, Augustus here has a new house to move into and I have beaches to lay out on!"

She scurried out of the kitchen. Sonny watched her go, then looked up at Augustus. "I'm glad to know the house will be well cared for. You've always liked it here, and you're like a second son to me." Only the latter part of his statement was false, though he didn't realize it. "I just want to make sure you know what you're getting yourself into. It's a big house and a lot of land, Augustus. Can you afford it?"

Insult instantly began to brim, but Augustus pushed it back. "Don't worry about me, Sonny. I've always got a plan." When Sonny nodded and gestured toward the stairs, indicating he was going to go help his wife pack, he offered a friendly smile and added, "And don't worry about the house, Sonny. I'll take good care of the place."

His former boss left him in the kitchen, rushing upstairs to pack. Augustus followed the man's progress with his eyes only, before letting them rove around the fully-upgraded kitchen free of water stains and chipped countertops and broken stoves, then to the large bay windows overlooking a landscaped backyard decorated with stone pavers surrounding a glistening fountain.

"Holy shit."

For one fleeting moment, Augustus felt panic for what he'd just done—lied to his former boss and his wife, essentially stealing their home right out from under them. Where would they go? Did their false memories come with an actual plan? How *would* he pay for this enormous house? How would it even legally be his?

You worry too much, said the spirit dwelling with him. *When you welcome the power, you welcome with it all the things you need to live a life of luxury.*

"It's not possible," he whispered back, feeling deep down that there had to be a flaw, a loophole where he would get caught and be thrown in prison. On what charges, he didn't know, but surely he was breaking at least one law here.

Accept the life you deserve, Augustus Jones. Accept me fully, take the gifts I have shown to you, and those yet to come, and never again will you find yourself wanting.

"Someone will suspect."

You have taken care of the nonbelievers, remember? Cleanse the city, you commanded. And so they did, before returning to the depths of Hell.

For a moment, Augustus had no idea what the demon was talking about. Then recent events filtered into his thoughts. The cemetery. The stupid teenagers and their foolish ritual. The call to darkness that brought forth the legion. And his command to them, one he hadn't even understood at the time—and still didn't.

With a deep, shuddering breath, Augustus asked, "Who were the nonbelievers?"

But there was no response. Only a hollow, aching emptiness foreshadowing a painful discovery.

CHAPTER 26

Augustus left his new home in a rush, not bothering to tell the former owners goodbye or ask for a key. Somehow, it would all be worked out by the time he returned tomorrow, he knew. Right now, he had to get to Mel.

Dread stabbed him straight in the gut with every step. He couldn't explain why, but instinct told him she was in danger. The Shax demon wouldn't have mentioned his command to the legion unless it wanted its host to know something. Augustus could only hope that *something* had nothing to do with the woman he thought he could one day love and marry.

A dozen times over he cursed himself for walking to Sonny's house as he ran to Mel's apartment. She lived close to the heart of Savannah, nowhere near what would be his new home, and he ran every mile of it, the thought to catch a cab never even occurring to him until he'd already stopped at the end of her street.

Even from the distance he could tell something was wrong. There was a small crowd huddled together on the sidewalk, along with a cluster of police cars and an ambulance blocking the narrow street. The atmosphere was somber, thick with curiosity and grief, so much so he could feel it growing stronger as he slowly approached the house where they all congregated. It was an older home, renovated into separate apartment units, and as he approached Augustus realized he could visualize the interior though he knew he'd never stepped foot inside.

More implanted memories, he figured.

No one noticed as he came to a stop at the back of the crowd. Augustus attempted to peer over their heads, trying to seem nonchalant though alarm and nervousness was eating through his gut. Tuning into their conversations, he heard words like "coroner" and "wonderful girl," and felt like he could vomit.

Movement at the front door had Augustus skirting the edge of the crowd until he stood closer to the ambulance. He watched two policemen exit first, followed by a paramedic guiding a stretcher. And on that stretcher was a black body bag.

"No." The single word was spoken on a gasp. Augustus didn't need to be told who was inside. His heart started to thump, so hard he pressed a hand to his chest, not able to pull his eyes away from the scene. Three more paramedics came out behind the stretcher, and there, at the end of the line, was Voodoo.

Augustus could barely wait until the ghost tour guide reached the sidewalk before grabbing hold of him. "Voodoo! What happened? Tell me that isn't…. Tell me it's not…."

But it was. The look in Voodoo's eyes, the grief written across his face, confirmed what Augustus already knew. He stumbled back a step, bracing himself on the white-picket fence, one hand scrubbing down his face.

"What happened, Voodoo?" he asked quietly, not wanting the nosy crowd to be any more part of the conversation than they already were. When the guide didn't answer, he looked up through tear-blurred vision to find Voodoo glaring at him. "What? Why are you looking at me like that?"

"Mel is dead," the man said plainly, his voice breaking on the word *dead*. His jaw clenched at the struggle for control, the shadows under his eyes accented by his black shirt and coat. He didn't seem to notice the single tear sliding down Augustus's face or the way he leaned over and gasped for air. "She took her own life."

At that, Augustus managed to look up, his body and mind shocked into focusing solely on Voodoo. "What? No. Mel would never do that."

"Except she did." Voodoo's tone turned hard, accusatory almost. "She slit her wrists, one at a time, deeper than any normal person should have been able to do. She locked her cat in the bathroom with enough food and water for a week, emptied out her bank account to pay off as much of her debts as possible, wrote her parents a goodbye note, then...then killed herself."

He heard the words, but his mind didn't want to accept them. Mel couldn't be dead. She never would have committed suicide. *Why* would she do such a thing? Grief struck his heart, nearly sending Augustus to his knees.

"This.... It doesn't make any sense. Mel would never do that. She...she was happy. She had goals. I don't...I don't understand." A thought occurred to him then and he stared at Voodoo with suspicion in his eyes. "How did you know what happened? Why were you inside?"

Voodoo breathed in deeply, collecting himself. "I was the one who found her." Then he closed his eyes, perhaps trying to cleanse his mind from the visual.

"But why were you here in the first place?" Augustus straightened, his grief turning to anger. Maybe he needed the deflection, or maybe he really was suspicious. Either way he wanted an answer.

"Why are you?"

Augustus's teeth grit together. "Answer the fucking question, Voodoo."

Instead of replying, Voodoo gave him the same wary stare from earlier. The two engaged in a face-off, both refusing to relent, neither willing to give up their secrets. All around them the crowd began to part now their show was over and the ambulance had driven away. Augustus was tempted to grab the other man by the neck when a throat cleared next to them.

"Mr. Burnheart," an officer spoke to Voodoo, "we'd like to ask you a few questions, just to document this for our paperwork. Would you be willing to speak with us over here?" He gestured to one of two remaining police cars.

"Absolutely," Voodoo replied, then to Augustus said, "Consider this my resignation, *boss*."

Augustus watched his retreating back, more confused than ever. Voodoo was accusing him of something, but had no idea what the hell those glares, not to mention his resignation, were hinting at.

"And why were you here?" he wondered aloud, searching his memories for any indication that Mel and Voodoo were more than just friends, jealousy rising to the surface despite finding nothing. His focus moved to the house, the top right window looking into Mel's bedroom. "Why would you do this, Mel?"

Cleanse the city, said the Shax. *Your legion does as commanded.*

Eyes wide, Augustus froze in place, heart barely beating. Cleanse the city, he'd ordered the thirty horsemen. A command to wipe Savannah clean of the ones whose minds could see through the veil in some small or large way, the ones who could have challenged him.

Cleanse the city, he'd demanded of his loyal legion. "I did this," he whispered, feeling the shame of his actions down to his core. "Mel...I'm so sorry."

*

The Will O'Wisp sensed the man's heartfelt sorrow from several streets over. It heard the sirens, had watched in its mind's eye as the distraught woman who thought she was going insane robotically scheduled her own death. And it knew the poor girl never stood a chance. Though she never saw it, a spirit on horseback had guided her every move, taking from her any understanding of what she was doing.

And now, she would be the first of Augustus Jones's many victims.

Soon Augustus would learn what it meant to allow a demon to reside within his body. He would learn that he, too, was just a foolish man playing with a ritual he did not understand. The Will O'Wisp held no sympathy for the man, one who was blinded by treasure and greed, but it did feel for his victims.

Savannah would soon discover the sins of the previous night. And the Will O'Wisp would be there through it all, watching, grieving, yet grateful it was all happening, because now it was one step closer to freedom.

CHAPTER 27

As soon as he stepped across the threshold of his house, he allowed the tears to fall. It wasn't tough or manly to cry, and unbecoming of a man of his rising stature, but he didn't care. All he could do was sit on the tattered couch with his head in his hands and weep for the girl he'd lost.

The girl he'd killed.

Somehow the legion, *his* legion, had found Mel in her home, traced her as someone who would one day threaten his reign, and removed her from the world. And they did it by making it look like a suicide. It was a murder of perfect, supernatural design, and it broke his heart.

He didn't know how long he sat there, but at some point Gert entered the room and took a seat next to him, never asking what was wrong, simply being there for her son. One frail arm wrapped around his shoulders and she held him like she used to do when he was a boy. Only when his tears subsided and he wiped his face did she speak.

"Tell me, my beautiful son. Tell me what's happened."

So he did, unloading the hurt onto her, telling Gert about Mel's death, about the grief he felt losing the woman he loved. Through the confession, he kept hidden the truth about her death, and when he was done Gert moved so she was holding his face in both hands.

"She was a good woman, and she knew how much you loved her. I know there is nothing I can say to make this hurt go away, but I will be here for you, my son. You let it all out, and I'll be right here."

Her devotion brought forth a small smile and he nodded. "Thank you, Mom. But I think I'd rather be alone."

Gert kissed his forehead and offered a lingering hug. "I understand, sweetie. You know where to find me." She got up slowly and ambled away, and only after she was gone did he remember forgetting to tell her about their new house.

"What's it matter?" he asked himself. It didn't, was his answer. None of it mattered anymore. This had all gone too far.

It will never go too far.

"Get out of my head," Augustus demanded, striking himself once in the center of the forehead. The move did nothing but anger him. "I never wanted Mel to die. I never wanted to confuse people like this. This was never supposed to happen."

You asked for it all to happen. Look, Augustus Jones. Look at what you have accomplished.

Of their own free will, his eyes moved to the television, his hand to the remote. He'd flicked the TV on and found the local news channel before he could even attempt to control his motions. A different woman was on the screen, likely a permanent replacement for Rebecca Wright after her curse-filled segment. This one was taller, with fiery red hair and large breasts currently on display in a tight-fitting blue dress.

Unlike Rebecca, who had been on the scene, the reporter was sitting at the desk with the anchorman. She turned to the camera, a box popping up in the upper right-hand corner as she spoke.

"Savannah was rocked today by the discovery of thirty suicides by local citizens across town."

Augustus sat up straighter, eyes instantly drying of tears and widening instead. He listened with a focus like never before as she continued, "Police and paramedics have been responding to calls all day from distraught family members and friends. With the sheer number of suicides in a single day, police are investigating each death, suspecting foul play and searching for anyone who may have any information as to why so many good men and women took their own lives within hours of one another."

The box in the corner shifted to a collage of faces. Augustus saw Mel in one of them, the picture bringing forth a fresh wave of sorrow. "Tonight, we remember our beloved community members, and cherish their lives. We would like to offer a moment of silence in their honor."

Both the reporter and the anchorman lowered their heads in respect. Augustus took the moment of silence to more closely observe the collage. There was Mel, so young and beautiful. There was a waitress from a local pub he'd flirted with from time to time, but couldn't remember her name. And, he noted with a sigh, there was Shelby Cross, his banker who suspected something was amiss with his savings account claim.

Shelby was a mother, a wife. She was a good woman who had done nothing except listen to his lie and try to help a client. "I'm so sorry, Shelby," he said to the screen, hating every part of himself and what he'd become.

Kings do not apologize.

"Shut up," Augustus retorted, just as the anchorman began to speak.

"Our hearts go out to everyone affected by these tragedies," the anchor said, "as they go out to the families in California affected by the mysterious fires and earthquakes that have ravaged towns."

A box popped up to the anchorman's left to show what Augustus assumed was California, homes leveled and an entire city on fire. "Officials are still trying to determine the source of these accidents, with the death toll now up in the hundreds."

Sighing, Augustus turned the TV off, not able to listen to any more depressing news. He just wanted to lock himself in his bedroom and try to figure out what to do next.

Tomorrow is a new day, Augustus Jones, the Shax spoke with glee. *The world is now yours for the taking.*

Ignoring the voice seeming to dictate his every move, Augustus rose and stalked to his bedroom, determined to sleep the misery away.

*

"Augustus? Wake up, honey."

Gert's voice filtered through the closed bedroom door, urgent and insistent. It took a moment for Augustus's eyes to open from a dreamless sleep. When they did, they were eyes seeing the world as they did the night at the cemetery, with a mind fighting against its newfound sight.

Groggily he rose and shuffled to the door, opening it just enough to see his mother. "What's wrong, Mom?"

"There are people at the door," she answered. "They say they are here to pack up our belongings. What's going on, Augustus?"

As though a switch flicked on in his head, Augustus remembered. "Today is moving day, Mother," he replied smoothly, all traces of sleep and irritation gone. "I wanted to surprise you—I bought us a new home. Get dressed and we'll head over shortly."

Not giving her time to protest or ask questions, Augustus closed the door and turned around, regarding his decrepit bedroom for what would be the last time. "Time for the king to return to his palace," he said with a grin.

Two hours later, they stood in their new living room, with its brick fireplace and plush leather couches, large entertainment center and smart TV his mother would never learn to use, and nautical-themed décor that gave the room a beachy feel.

Gert turned a slow circle, taking it all in with a smile. She'd already seen her new first-floor bedroom, which was double the size of her former room, and marveled over the kitchen. "Augustus, this is amazing," she breathed, her hands clasping together in delight. "So beautiful."

"And safe," he agreed. "No more walls that are falling down or mold in the attic. No more broken appliances. No more backyard overrun with weeds and fire ants. A new home that you deserve."

'But, Augustus, how can you afford this?" Her excitement faded slightly. Gert walked to the window, peering out at the pool and gardens. "It's such a big house and yard. Isn't this too expensive? How did you buy this home?"

With a wave of his hand, Augustus replied, "Don't worry about that, Mom. I told you, I have a plan. I've been saving, and business has been good. This is all taken care of."

She believed his lie, as he'd known she would. With her worry appeased, Augustus placed a hand on her shoulder and started guiding her to her bedroom. "Why don't you take a nap? I need to get ready. Mel's church has organized a gathering for her tonight, and it's important I be there."

CHAPTER 28

He arrived late, purposely stalling to avoid prolonged small talk with people he knew would want to reminisce. For a while he simply stood outside the church, sneering up at the cross rising high above the rooftop, staring at stained-glass windows depicting scenes from Christ's birth. There were few things he wanted to do less than enter that church, with the pain from losing Mel still far too fresh.

Or maybe it's not my hesitation at all, he thought bitterly, feeling the resistance within his mind and blood. It was starting to ache, this constant sensation of not being alone, as though a band was being wrapped around his heart, tightening a little more each day. Worse, he was starting not to care. It was fun at first, being given everything his heart desired in exchange for allowing an alleged demon access to his soul. It wasn't like he believed it were real, anyway. But now it was a chore, keeping track of who was told what lie and how that lie was now affecting his life.

"Let's see how you like it," he growled, then purposely strode up the steps and into the church. His body felt like it was trying to rip itself in two as he crossed the threshold and he couldn't help the whimper of pain that escaped. His gut roiled, heart pounded, teeth grit together in resistance. Still he persisted until the door closed behind him, pushing back the feelings of hate and trepidation until he felt himself—his *real* self—regaining control.

Though, he couldn't help but wonder how much of that control was an illusion.

The celebration of Mel's life had been quickly organized only a day after her passing, but the turnout was large; more than half the church was filled to remember the woman who brought joy to so many lives. From the back of the church, Augustus saw people he'd known for years as associates in the ghost tour industry, but also tourists who were still in town and had joined Mel on a tour throughout Savannah earlier in the week.

It was an informal gathering, he noted, but no less thoughtful. Even from the back he could see the many pictures spread throughout the small church, with a large print propped up on an easel at the front altar. Mourners milled about, some with drinks in hand, others with tissues.

"Augustus. Thank you for joining us."

Pulling his eyes away from the pictures and mourners, Augustus saw Pastor Raymond Wiles standing to his right. He wore a sad, gloomy expression, though was obviously trying to remain cheerful for the others.

"Of course," he replied, filling his voice with grief he actually felt, and sympathy he didn't. "Mel was...."

"I know how important she was to you," Raymond finished, mistaking Augustus's inability to finish the sentence for something other than what it was—an internal war between spirit and soul for control. "You made her so happy. I only wish we could have known she was in so much pain."

"Unless it was all part of a greater plan." Internally, Augustus cringed and cursed at the demon taking control of his motor functions. *Shut the fuck up,* he ordered, but the Shax wasn't listening, and was growing impatient with its host's need to maintain his own mind. Before the pastor could reply, he continued, "Thirty suicides in one night. Sometimes I wonder if Mel was part of something we never knew about. Something dark and dangerous. And that maybe they meant for this to happen all along."

Uncomfortable now, Raymond looked down at his feet, then up at the ceiling, brow furrowing. "Are you saying this was planned? That so many people meant to rip their loved ones' lives apart by taking their own, all for some greater spiritual purpose?"

Augustus lifted a shoulder. "Perhaps. Or perhaps they found a darkness they didn't understand and couldn't control, and paid the price." It was a message within a message, though Raymond would never know that. The pastor simply frowned and offered a brief condolence before excusing himself and hurrying away.

Augustus followed the man's hasty retreat, until his gaze landed on Voodoo and Silas. The two were standing along the opposite wall, Voodoo with his arms crossed, Silas gripping a cup. Both had their glares aimed directly at him. Squaring his shoulders, Augustus crossed the church, ignoring condolences from those he passed, and came to a stop in front of the guides.

"Gentlemen," he greeted. "Thanks for coming. I'm sure it would mean a lot to Mel to have us all here."

"Cut this shit, Jones," Voodoo replied. His voice was low so only they could hear. "We both know you have no business being here."

Augustus frowned, both man and demon trying to determine what the man meant. "And why is that?"

"You should go," Silas said in answer. His usual happy-go-lucky attitude was gone, replaced by a somber seriousness. "I'm sure it would mean a lot to Mel for you to leave."

They know something, the Shax whispered to its host, an unspoken demand to know what, only Augustus had no idea. All he knew was that these two were staring at him like he'd killed Mel with his own two hands, and were now all but ordering him to leave the church, like he wasn't allowed to mourn for the woman he'd wanted to call his own since the moment he first met her.

How dare they, he grumbled internally. How dare they look at him like he was some common criminal. How dare they assume the authority to order him to do anything. They were mere tour guides. His employees. He was Augustus fucking Jones.

You take orders from no man.

Augustus set his jaw, the simple move eliciting a glimmer of hesitation in the men before him. Out of the corner of his eye he observed the others. Several were watching the trio, the pastor included. So many eyes on him.

"This isn't how it's supposed to go," Augustus spoke, wincing when he realized he said the words out loud.

Great things come to those who never stray from the path, said the demon, just as Voodoo replied, "Whatever way it was supposed to go, it's all about to end."

"Just go, man," Silas agreed. "Don't make this messier than it has to be."

Even greater things come to those who let others think they have won.

Augustus released a deep breath, eyes narrowing but mouth remaining closed against all the things he wanted to say. Instead of arguing, he merely turned on his heel and strode out of the church, stopping when his foot touched the rickety wood deck, which vibrated beneath him.

He knew that feeling. It scared him, just as much as it thrilled him. A stork landed on the fence separating church from sidewalk and trained its vision on Augustus, who kept his breath steady as he stared back, the smallest of nods the only acknowledgement.

From his peripheral he saw dark figures rise up from the earth. It was a quick calling, mere seconds, then he heard the clomping of hooves on the church deck sounding until they stopped a few feet away, warmth from a torch warming the side of his face.

"Cleanse the church," Augustus said to the horseman without turning his head, then took the six steps down the church entrance. He walked slowly to the road, and, though he couldn't see what was happening behind him, he knew nonetheless. In his mind, he could see the horsemen surrounding the building, and then, one by one, torches lowered.

When he reached the street, Augustus turned slowly, purposefully, grinning when he saw the smoke starting to rise into a cloudless blue sky. A chorus of screams met his ears next and he closed his eyes to bask in it, listening to their terror, enjoying the thuds of fists on closed windows and doors.

His eyes opened when one of those doors splintered. The horsemen were gone, but the church was ever present, burning from the ground up. Flames licked up from the base, sliding up to the windows, kissing the eaves with sparkling embers. A window fractured and erupted from the heat, black smoke billowing out in tumbling waves, just as the front door was finally thrust open, broken apart by a pew shoved through the wood.

People began stumbling out, covering their soot-smudged faces with jackets and shirts, some helping drag out those who were too weak to run. One child was passed out; another woman had a burn mark on her left cheek. All were coughing and dry heaving.

Augustus hid a smile as he took it all in. Mourners rushed past him, not even noticing that he stood in place with his arms behind his back, refusing to back away from the burning building, not afraid or surprised. The last of the crowd fell down the steps, all but crawling away from the church just as sirens rang out a few streets over. But by the time they arrived, it would be too late. The church was burning at an almost unnatural pace, the flames searing and growing higher by the second, smoke filling the sky. A fire truck rounded the corner at the end of the road. Only then did Augustus move, narrowing his eyes at the vehicle, then at the man who stepped into his line of vision.

"You did this," Voodoo snarled hoarsely. "I don't know how, but you did this. And you won't get away with it."

"I did nothing." His tone was nonchalant, bored even. "It is your pastor you should be accusing. He is the one who burned down his own church."

Voodoo stepped back, wiping a hand down his smudged face and smearing black across his cheeks. "What? Why would Pastor Raymond...." One glance over his shoulder at the church, then at the surrounding crowd of coughing people, brought forth a terrible truth—Pastor Raymond was nowhere to be found. "No... He didn't make it out!"

Voodoo began to race back into the church, but Silas grabbed him by the arm, thrusting him back onto the sidewalk. "No! You can't go back in there!"

"He'll die if we don't help!"

"He is already dead." This was said by a stoic Augustus. "A captain must go down with his ship."

"You heartless son of a bitch," Voodoo whispered, but his reply fell on deaf ears, for a portly and red-faced man in uniform had approached and captured Augustus's attention.

"Mr. Jones," the man began, "my name is Detective Winston Blake. I have some questions for you. Would you mind coming with me back to the station?"

Voodoo smirked. "Like I said. You won't get away with this." Then he and Silas backed away, moving to help the others, satisfied their former boss was in the hands of the law.

"Right this way, Mr. Jones," Detective Blake said with a gesture toward his squad car. Augustus merely looked down at his hand, then back up at the man.

"I believe earlier you said we would be fine speaking right over here. That there was no need to go down to the station. After all, we're friends, and you always give me the benefit of the doubt." Instead of going to the car, he walked a few paces away from prying eyes and ears, giving the duo privacy beneath an oak tree. It didn't block their view of the church, with flames still burning bright despite the firemen's best attempts, but it did afford the quiet Augustus needed.

"What can I help you with, Blake?" he asked before Blake could try to piece together what he'd actually said and what his brain was now reconfiguring.

Blake blinked his dark-brown eyes several times, running a hand over closely cropped black hair, then came back to the moment. "Yes, yes. Of course. I wanted to get the facts before letting anyone else talk to you and possibly bring you into the station for questioning."

"Questioning about what?"

"About Shelby Cross."

At the name, Augustus tried to school his features but it was a second too late. Hesitation was clear in his voice when he asked, "What about her?"

"As I'm sure you know, Savannah was hit hard with the thirty suicides the other night. Shelby Cross was one of them."

Augustus nodded cautiously. "I did. Such a tragedy."

"Did you know her well?"

"Somewhat. She was my banker. Why do you ask?"

Blake shifted, taking a moment to watch the firemen at work, the blazing church, paramedics assisting those who had escaped the flames. It was chaos all around them, but, he noted with interest, Augustus didn't seem bothered by any of it.

"As part of the investigation into the suicides, Miss Cross's files were looked into. We found she had made a call to your cell phone not long before her death, and that she had a file on her computer with your banking information in it. Any idea why she would be making this file?"

The expectant look on the detective's face told Augustus the man already knew the answer. "Why don't you tell me, Blake?"

"Why don't you tell me about the money she transferred into

your personal savings account, just days before you purchased a business from Sonny Harvest?"

Shit, Augustus thought, trying to think of a lie. He couldn't tell the truth, and didn't know enough about his new life to seamlessly integrate an influx of money, especially since he had no idea what kind of information Shelby was actually gathering on him.

You need only allow me to answer, said the voice in his head, an invitation to succumb, a promise for escape.

"Augustus? Please give me a rational explanation. I don't want to have to bring you in."

Again he searched for a response, frustrated his mind was so distressingly blank. As though something was blocking his ability to formulate words, he considered.

There is an escape. There is also a cell, trapping you for life from all the fortune you deserve.

He wouldn't go to prison. Not for Shelby Cross. Not for anyone.

"Miss Cross was my banker, but we also had a more personal relationship a few years ago, if you understand my meaning," Augustus claimed, his eyes staring straight into Blake's, unblinking and even. "It was a private relationship, in that we didn't want many people to know, given I was her client and that she was married, but it ended with us as friends. Soon after, I began seeing Mel, and Shelby apparently didn't take it well. I'd thought we could remain friends and professionals, but a few months ago she started suggesting we rekindle our relationship. I refused, given that I was with Mel. She'd been upset, and hinted she wouldn't take the rejection lightly."

Here he blew out a breath and shook his head. "I never imagined she would make up information about me, all to get back at me for a failed relationship." His stare zeroed in on Blake even more. "You understand, I'm sure. As they say, hell hath no fury like a woman scorned. Shelby has been attempting to frame me for theft. Her suicide is a result of the guilt she felt in trying to have me put in prison for unjustified reasons."

Blake's lips had parted in shock as Augustus spoke. It was almost comical, Augustus thought, the way the detective's mouth gaped like a fish, perhaps in tune with every cell in his body being rearranged to suit a new world with a new set of knowledge.

But Augustus wasn't done yet. "Just two days ago, you and I discussed some sort of cease and desist order being delivered to her, since you were helping me look into why I was getting so many alerts on my credit for accounts being opened or otherwise tampered with. Shelby was the cause of those too, attempting to destroy my finances in order to prevent the purchase of my business and future home. I am extremely appreciative of all your help, Blake, and hope we can put this all past us."

A shout had both men looking back to the church in time to see the roof cave in. The sight sucked the detective back into the scene and his body jerked slightly in surprise. He took in each scene one by one—the church now in flaming pieces, the mourners huddled together in smoke-smudged clumps or sitting on the curb with heads between their knees, policemen talking to witnesses, and Augustus standing next to an oak tree looking decidedly unaffected.

Seeming to come to a conclusion, Blake nodded. "Okay.... This has all been a very strange few days."

"That it has," Augustus agreed good-naturedly.

"I'll let you go, and do apologize for taking up your time with this nonsense. I'll have the paperwork filled out this afternoon to make sure your name is cleared of Shelby Cross's mess. In the meantime, make sure you speak with one of the officers about the fire. They will want to speak with everyone who was in the church."

Blake walked away, leaving Augustus to consider his request. In the distance he saw one officer speaking to Voodoo, and both were looking his way. "Not today," he muttered, then began to back toward the street. In the rush of firemen and spectators and general chaos, he was able to slip away, strolling briskly until he was two streets over and protected by several rows of houses.

The farther he got from the fire, the more Augustus felt like himself. He could physically sense the Shax retreating, the fog around his mind lifting, replaced by something far worse—fear. Fear for what was happening to him, what he'd *let* happen. Fear for who he was becoming. And fear for the truth, that what Jason told him was actually possible, and the house on Abercorn really was a place of evil paranormal activity.

"The house," he whispered, glancing at the street sign to get his bearings, then running toward Abercorn until the house of his nightmares came into view. It looked so innocent in the daylight, just a house in need of fresh paint and maybe a gardener or two.

"A wolf in sheep's clothing," he said to himself, then checked his sides for potential witnesses. There were none—everyone was at the church, watching the day's entertainment in the form of a tragedy. Then he squared his shoulders and did what he said he'd never do again.

He went back inside the house.

CHAPTER 29

Augustus felt the chill in the air as soon as he entered. An unnatural chill, one that spoke of danger soon to come. He didn't stop to peer around at the décor or pretend he didn't know where he was going. His feet brought him straight to the hallway in the back of the house. There were no windows here, no light. Just the gaping black void signaling the loss of one's soul.

"I know you're here," Augustus said into the darkness, but his forceful tone was countered by the shock of hearing his voice come out with an Irish accent. That was the accent reserved for his tours, for his persona.

Clearing his throat, he tried again to speak in his normal American tone. "I know you're here."

Again the Irish brogue came out of its own accord. Cursing to himself, Augustus let the fake accent continue with his next words. "I know the Will O'Wisp dwells here in this hallway, so let's get on with it." He could feel another's presence, just as he could sense the demon slowly overtaking his own soul as it resisted being back in the place where it was trapped for so long. "Let's not drag this out. I have a bone to pick with you, and you're going to answer all my fucking questions."

Icy-cold air blew in from the end of the hall. Augustus stood his ground, though he couldn't help the way his body tightened and breath trembled out of him. And then he saw it—an outline against the shadows steadily creeping forward, lit only by the single flame burning brighter than any light ever should.

His heart pounded against his chest and he knew, he *knew*, if he saw this thing up close and personal, he would never be the same. "Stop. Don't come any closer," Augustus ordered. It was bad enough, knowing some kind of light-bearing creature lived in the house he'd showed eager tourists for more than ten years. Seeing its face would surely send him into complete insanity.

"You have come for answers," it spoke as it stopped, its voice surprisingly soft and friendly. "They all seek answers."

"...They?" Augustus repeated after a pause, hating how nervous he sounded. "Who are they?"

"Those who enter into the bid. They all come back when they realize what is happening. You have lasted longer than most, Augustus Jones. Your curiosity has not been as strong as the others."

Oh, his curiosity is strong, the demon within laughed in response. *But his curiosity lies in the fortunes he craves.*

Not sure if the hallway spirit heard the voice in his head, Augustus cleared his throat and asked, "What's happening to me?"

"You already know the answer, Augustus Jones."

"The bid, the big, bad bet over who will win whose soul," he assumed, sarcasm thick in his tone. "Jason Waters told me what you do, that you host demons within yourself and let them, what? Possess people just because they come into the house? It's absurd. It's not.... It's not real."

"Then how do you explain speaking to me? How do you explain the time you cannot remember when standing in this very same spot?" The questions were asked softly, gently. "If it is not real, then what is it?"

He didn't have a reply, didn't want to search for one lest he find an answer he couldn't accept. So, Augustus tried a different question. "Why would you do this? What did I ever do to deserve this? Why is this happening?"

"Why," it mused, not coming closer but shifting in place, what Augustus guessed was the head nearly touching the ceiling. The light blazed brighter before dimming mildly. "You all want to know why. You all want to believe it was chance, or bad luck, or fate turning against you. Tell me, Augustus Jones, will the *why* truly make you feel better?"

He wanted to retort with a sarcastic or furious reply, but inside, Augustus had to admit the truth. It wouldn't matter, why this was happening. And, worse, he already knew the answer. He went into a house that wasn't his. He allowed a voice in his mind to dictate his actions. He chose to accept the gifts given to him as bribes. And he always wanted more.

Ask the real questions, spoke the inner voice, a taunt more than a suggestion. *Discover the truth among the lies you've told.*

"Fine," he relented with a sigh. "Then tell me why this didn't happen the first time I came into the house with Jason."

"You weren't ready the night you rescued Jason Waters. You were just a man helping someone in need."

"What changed?"

The spirit moved in a way Augustus guessed was a shrug. "You saw the power Jason Waters was given, the fame and fortune earned by his great discovery and healing of the world, and you wanted it for yourself."

He wanted to argue, but couldn't deny the truth of the statement. Even though he'd been terrified that night he and Jason dug up the graves of yellow fever victims, he'd also been in awe of the man who healed overnight and went on to achieve great things. There *had* been times when Augustus was jealous, when he wanted those things for himself—the wealth, the recognition—no matter how he had to get them.

He'd brought this upon himself.

Yes, the demon agreed with a gleeful hiss. *Now you accept the truth of your greatest lie.*

Augustus sighed again and leaned against the wall, suddenly needing the support. "So all this happened because I was stupid enough to come in here a second time." If only he'd stayed out, he could have lived his life free of influence. Mel would still be alive. Shelby Cross would be alive and with an untarnished name. Sonny and his wife would be in their home, not traveling across the country to fate unknown. Pastor Raymond, a good man, wouldn't have burned to death in his own church.

And he'd still be Nathaniel Jones, lowly ghost tour guide with no money, a falling-apart house, and no future to look forward to. A nobody with no reason to respect himself or his life.

Stop it, he ordered himself, hating that, despite everything, he still wanted the future promised to him. Worse, he couldn't deny that if given the chance again, he would make the same choice.

In response, his inner demon whispered, *We all make sacrifices for the things we want most.*

Ignoring the Shax, Augustus thought back to the night he entered this house for the second time, and a disturbing question came to mind. "Wait. The girl, Hayden, she was with me. She's why I came into the house again. What happened to her?"

"Worry not for the child," the Will O'Wisp replied. "She will be taken care of."

"What does that mean?" When he didn't get a reply, Augustus lifted a hand to his forehead, rubbing away the beginnings of a headache. "What am I supposed to do now? Everything is out of control. The woman I love is dead, and it's because of me. My own mother no longer knows who I really am. The whole world is fucking up and I can't make it stop. How do I make it stop?"

"You don't." The Will O'Wisp sounded resigned to that fact. "You have entered into the bid, Augustus Jones, and the bid has been settled. You accepted the offering, and now you must also accept your fate."

Steeling himself against the response, Augustus crossed his arms, jaw set despite the twitch in his fingers. "And if I reject that fate?"

Now the spirit sighed, mimicking his. "Then you lose yourself completely."

*

Lose yourself completely.

The words rang in his mind the entire way home. It didn't go unnoticed by him that he immediately and instinctively went to his new house, letting himself in through the back to avoid his mother. The back area opened up into a small mudroom, where he supposed one should take off their shoes after a tennis game, or maybe strip out of a wet bathing suit and hang it up on one of the many hooks in the wall. There was also a large sink and drying rack.

The mudroom led to the laundry room, with so fancy a washer and dryer set he knew Gert would never figure it out. He'd have to write down instructions for her, or find someone to do the laundry for her. Just past the laundry room was the set of stairs he wanted, a narrow set leading up to the second floor where he'd chosen his room.

Walking down the long, wide hallway, Augustus thought of all the ways he'd redecorate if given the time. The gaudy orange walls would have to go, replaced by cool blues reminiscent of the sea. Likewise, the city-themed décor would be replaced, with fewer framed pictures of New York City and San Francisco and more knickknacks that reminded him of the beach. Maybe even a few pictures of Savannah and its famous River Street.

But it didn't matter. He would never get the chance to see his visions come to live.

When he reached his room, Augustus closed and locked the door, taking a moment to lean against it, forehead pressed to the wood. His whole body hummed with anticipation, pain building behind his eyes as he tried desperately to block his thoughts from the Shax.

"I'm sorry, Mom," he whispered, then pushed himself off the door and stalked into the private bathroom. It was roomy and light, with pale-pink tile and off-white walls, a marble double sink, and separate glass shower and spa-style tub.

A bathroom fit for a man of your stature, the demon claimed, a clear attempt to butter up its host.

But it wouldn't work, Augustus determined. "Get out of my head," he ordered, closing the bathroom door. "Get out of my body. Get out of my life. Find someone else to haunt."

Oh, but Augustus Jones, we have already had such fun together.

The croaky, hoarse voice grated on his nerves. His last nerve, not that he had any left to spare. "Shut the fuck up. This isn't fun. You killed Mel."

I did no such thing, Augustus Jones. You commanded the legion to cleanse the city, not I.

"Because you made me." At the sink, Augustus stared at himself in the mirror. He saw the same face he'd known for thirty-five years, watched it mature over the years into the charming façade that easily charmed women. From a young age Augustus had known he was handsome, and often used his looks to get what he wanted—jobs, girls, an excuse to get out of trouble.

Now, he hated his face. It wasn't his own. His eyes were the same dark brown, hair the same style, the scar above his lip from a childhood bout with chicken pox. But it wasn't his face. There was a smoothness to it, a glow even. A clear sign he was no longer in possession of his soul. Maybe other people couldn't see it, but he could.

And it was going to stop.

Augustus opened drawer after drawer in the large bathroom until he found what he was looking for: a pair of scissors with sharp tips and blades. Without thinking, he crawled into the tub and lay back. Regret and sorrow ate at his heart as he thought of all the things he was giving up, but above it all was hope—hope that *he* would win, and not the evil spirit that invaded his dreams and thought it could bid for his soul.

The blade hovered over his wrist. With the move, his thoughts could no longer be blocked from the demon, which understood exactly what its host intended to do. *You cannot do this, Augustus Jones.*

"Like hell I can't," he grumbled in reply. "If you're going to take my soul without permission, then I'm going to take it back."

What of your unfinished business? The instructions for your mother on washing her clothes?

"She'll figure out it." But even as he replied, he felt fresh guilt pour over him in a wave.

Your good name will be tarnished. Blasted in your nightly news, your reputation disrespected across the nation.

"I'll be dead. What do I care?" Augustus heard the desperation in the demon's voice, relished in it. Let the spirit worry. Let it fear going back to its prison in the house on Abercorn Street.

"I will not lose myself completely to you," he growled, then lowered the scissors to his wrist and pressed blade against skin.

CHAPTER 30

Blood was expected, but only pristine, uncut skin stared up at Augustus.

He tried again, a rapid movement to slice scissor against wrist, but his arm wouldn't cooperate, hovering an inch above his skin, refusing to lower. Will battled against will in the effort to slice his own wrist open, his hand shaking against an invisible force preventing him from doing so.

You will not do this, Augustus Jones, said the Shax. *You will not leave your body to bleed out for your mother to find.*

"Like hell I won't," he replied on a snarl, sitting forward and hunching over. The closer quarters forced his arms together, but still he couldn't make contact. Involuntarily, his fingers relaxed and the scissors fell to the tub with a clatter.

"Son of a bitch." With a frustrated shout, Augustus pushed himself up from the tub and stomped out of the bathroom in search of a new weapon. He pawed through what was left of Sonny and Barb's belongings—which was most of them, since they hadn't yet sent the movers—finally finding what he wanted on the top shelf of the closet.

"Let's see you fight this." Opening the plastic gun case, Augustus made quick work of loading the revolver. Without bothering to find a good final resting place, he put the gun to his head and pulled the trigger.

Or, tried to, anyway.

Like with the knife, his hand wouldn't obey the command his brain was ordering. "Come on. Come on!" he shouted through gritted teeth, his entire arm shaking against the effort to pull the trigger and end his possessed life.

But he couldn't do it. Augustus threw the gun to the floor and buried his head in his hands. Too many thoughts rushed at him at once—his stupid decision to track a surly teenager into a haunted house, the dreams of spirits trying to win him over to their side, the first promise of fortune sucking him in, a new life filled with riches and the woman of his dreams, and it all taken away with his command to the legion.

So much hurt, the Shax said. *So much pain and confusion you need not feel.*

"Stop it," Augustus whispered, not able to bear the memories, the reality of what he'd done over the last few days. Had it really only been a week's time? Seven days in which his world changed, Mel died, he stole a business and home from a good man, and he burned down a church for no real reason at all.

"I didn't do those things. It wasn't me. It wasn't me." The words continued to flow, quiet mutterings from a man quickly losing control.

Let me take away the pain.

He didn't know who he was anymore. Nathaniel Jones? Augustus Jones? Both, or just one? Was he an honorable man with a decent job who flirted with women on occasion, or was he a snake lying in wait, who would rearrange women's memories to make them think they were lovers?

Augustus looked at the gun, wanting to grab it, wanting to blow his brains out all over the fucking wall, but his arms wouldn't move. He looked up at the ties hanging neatly on a rack in the closet and thought briefly of looping them around his neck, but just as the image came to mind it fizzled out.

"I can't do it," he said to himself, not giving up by choice, but by influence. The Shax wasn't willing to lose its host and be sent back to the Will O'Wisp to lie in wait for another poor soul, so it was making sure this one stayed alive.

"I can't do it," he said again, this time a confession to the life he couldn't live. He couldn't be the man who lied to change his fate, altering the world and minds of those around him. "I'm better than this."

If you were, said the Shax, *then the bid would never have been won.*

"Shut up." Augustus pounded a fist against his head, enjoying the pain, wanting it to hurt more. "Just shut up." Again he struck himself, finally able to do something to cause damage, even if it was just a bruise or headache.

An idea surfaced, and before he could let it formulate in his mind, Augustus leapt to his feet and ran into the bathroom. And, not letting himself think, rammed head-first into the large full-body mirror on the wall.

Glass shattered, falling to the tile in razor-sharp chunks. Blood dripped from sparkling shards, pooling in sticky puddles, reflecting off the bright overhead lights in a crimson ocean. Augustus didn't notice any of it. He slumped to the floor with a groan, landing on his back and staring up at the swirls of paint coating the ceiling with blurred vision.

Another moan tumbled from his lips, his voice cracking as his body shifted atop the fallen glass, but he couldn't find the coordination to rise. His head throbbed too much, feeling like his brain would burst out of his skull.

Is this what it feels like to die? Augustus asked himself, relief overtaking the pain. If it was, he would welcome every second of it and let it happen, if it meant not letting the demon win. So he forced his body to lie still, concentrating on the feel of hot blood seeping out of his forehead, his heart beating slower and slower as he relaxed, the soothing hum of a running air conditioner lulling him to sleep.

*

His eyes opened. The first thing they saw was the ceiling with its fancy swirls of paint before they closed again, taking stock of everything else. A forehead with an unbelievable amount of pain stabbing through it. Skin that felt as sticky as it did filthy. A back aching with the dozens of glass shards stabbing into it.

"Fuck," Augustus muttered, lifting a hand to his eyes and wiping away the blood blurring his vision. His entire face was wet. Disgust curdled within him. With a sigh, he slowly rose to a sitting position, hand never leaving his head, fighting a wave of nausea that threatened to send him back to the floor.

The wave passed after a moment, allowing him to rise to his knees, glass shifting and crunching beneath his weight. He gripped the counter for support, needing something solid to hold onto with every inch he rose. When he was finally straightened, Augustus lifted his head and witnessed the damage done in the mirror above the sink.

His forehead was littered with holes, a collage of glass and dirt spread from temple to temple in one bloody painting. There were several impact points, all oozing blood or starting to scab over—he must have been passed out for a while, he noted. Bruises were forming around his eyes and temples, further darkened by the blood dripping down the sides of his face, either side of his nose, around the corners of his mouth.

Fighting a wince, Augustus leaned over and turned the warm water on, filling his hands and splashing water on his face. It hurt, more than he'd thought it would, earning him another round of nausea. Grabbing the towel hanging next to the sink, he opted for that route instead, slowly, painstakingly, wiping away the blood everywhere but his forehead. Only when his face was clean did he start the process of pulling chunks of glass from his skin.

"Son of a bitch," he grumbled, tugging a particularly large piece out from above his temple and dropping it to the sink, which had quickly filled with pieces of glass mixed with spots of blood.

It took the better part of an hour to clean himself, and only when he was done did Augustus allow himself to leave the bathroom. His face was clean, if not bruised and scabbed, and now his soiled clothes needed to go.

Pawing through the closet, Augustus selected a fresh set of clothes from the minimal items he'd brought—Sonny's leftovers were far too large—and dressed just as slowly as he'd cleaned himself. Even his body ached, which surprised him.

"Such a fool," he said with a shake of his head.

Tossing his bloody clothes into the corner of the closet, Augustus straightened his collared shirt and caught a glimpse of himself in another mirror above the dresser. He looked refined, save for the mess that was his forehead.

Who am I? The question formed without warning, worried words running across the front of his thoughts.

He smiled at his reflection, a slow and calculated grin matched by narrowed eyes. When he answered the question, it was with a voice low and raspy, a testament to a soul powerless to save itself.

"I am Augustus Jones."

*

It felt the moment the takeover occurred. From the darkest shadow of the hallway, the Will O'Wisp sighed, curled into a ball and trying to sleep away the guilt of another man losing his life.

Losing his mind, it corrected. Tessa Taylor and Jason Waters had been stronger than Augustus, able to co-exist with their demons in a way that gave them all exactly what they wanted. But Augustus

Jones couldn't handle the truth of what happened, couldn't accept the life that came with such a relationship.

Or maybe Augustus was the stronger one, the Will O'Wisp considered. He was given everything he ever dreamed of, yet was willing to throw it all away in order to take back the control that had been ripped away from him. He tried to end his life, but, in doing so, lost only his mind instead.

The Will O'Wisp closed its eyes, ignoring the bright burn of the single flame left on its hand. It didn't want to think about the pain it had caused. Not tonight.

Tonight was for mourning the death of Nathaniel Jones.

CHAPTER 31

Only when he felt calm and collected did Augustus leave the bedroom, making his way throughout the house with slow, deliberate steps. Walking like a man would walk, observing a new house with unfamiliar décor, memorizing details Augustus Jones would and should know.

He entered the kitchen, seeing the woman he knew as Gert Jones sitting at the table with a newspaper in front of her. She didn't notice him at first, so he took a moment to observe the woman. Old and frail, he saw, with a face folded with wrinkles, thin and curled gray hair, and gnarled hands signifying limited use of her limbs.

Decidedly not a threat, he decided, and took a few more steps so she would sense his presence.

Bright blue eyes lifted to meet his, shock filling them. Gert rose with a stifled cry, rushing to her son and gently taking hold of his face, turning it left and right to survey the damage.

"What happened?" she gasped, barely able to get the words out around the tears already filling her eyes and sob stuck in her throat. "Who did this to you?"

Augustus took her hands in his own and lowered them, smiling down at her. "It's nothing, Mother. Just an accident. I've already been to the doctor and he says everything is fine. Just need some time to heal and make this face handsome again." His grin widened and he winked, getting a chuckle out of Gert.

"There's my Augustus I know and love," she said with a soft pat to his cheek. "You really are a rascal."

You have no idea, Gert Jones, he thought, watching her return to the table and pick up her pen to resume the crossword.

"Oh, honey," Gert looked up again, "I forgot. How silly of me! Two of your friends are in the living room. They asked to speak with you right away. I can't believe I forgot. Please apologize to them for me."

"Of course." Augustus looked toward the doorway, searching for memories of which direction the living room was in, all the while wondering who the two friends were and what they wanted. Gert forgetting they were there likely had worked in his favor, given he was passed out on the bathroom floor for who knew how long.

"Stay here, Mother," he said before heading out. "We have business to discuss so we don't want to be disturbed."

Gert waved a hand at him, absorbed in her crossword, and he trusted she would do as told. He found his way to the living room and paused just outside the door, taking in a deep breath and preparing himself for what he hoped would be friendly conversation rather than confrontation.

A dark-haired man stood in the center of the room, shoulders tense and expression one of carefully crafted control. His black shirt and pants matched the somber mood in the room. "Voodoo," Augustus greeted from the doorway, the man-turned-demon remembering the ghost tour guide and their encounters over the last few days. "What are you doing here?"

He stepped into the room, approaching the other man, who still hadn't said a word. It wasn't until a scuffle sounded behind him that he realized they weren't alone. Turning, Augustus saw the other guide, *Silas,* his memory told him, rising to his feet. Wondering why the dreadlocked man had been on his knees, Augustus looked down.

His breath caught in his throat when he saw the small triangle he stood in. Three sides made of gnarled pieces of wood that were, he noted with both amusement and disgust, dipped in holy water. He could smell the almost angelic scent. The water didn't have the power to hold him, and it humored him that these mere peasants thought it would, but the triangle the wood formed did. He was effectively trapped.

Refusing to show weakness or fear, Augustus straightened his back and stared straight at Voodoo. "What are you doing? What is the meaning of this?"

"I'll be the one asking the questions," Voodoo retorted. "Who are you?"

"I am Augustus Jones." His voice came out smooth, melodic, as it always was when speaking the truth.

Silas and Voodoo exchanged a wary glance, one that interested Augustus. They hadn't been expecting his answer. Not to be deterred, Voodoo pulled a piece of paper out of his pocket and unfolded it, then held it up in front of his prisoner. "Do you know what this is?"

A quick glance at the paper gave him his reply. "No."

"You asked me why I was at Mel's place the day she died. *This* is why. *This* is the meaning of today, and why we're doing this." Voodoo turned the paper around and began to read. "Voodoo, I don't know why I'm writing this or why I'm about to do what I'm going to do. I feel so confused, like something is making me remember a life I never knew, yet I still know it. I know that doesn't make sense, but I hope you'll believe me when I tell you something is wrong."

Here he paused, glaring up at Augustus, who nodded thoughtfully. *A strong mortal to resist the illusion*, he considered, then saw Voodoo wasn't done.

"Augustus isn't himself. I have this memory, or maybe it was a dream, where he told me people believed anything he said and he thought he was going crazy. He was scared, but then later, he wasn't, like he'd accepted it and I was the crazy one, not him. I did some research. I know it sounds insane, but there is a demon named the Shax. The Shax is faithful to the one who conjures it, but it also a great liar and will deceive everyone, including its host. It will only speak the truth when trapped in a triangle drawn on the floor. This is the only time you can get honest answers and know you aren't being deceived. And the Shax is also known for giving people great treasures. Voodoo, I know it's crazy and sounds like something we would put in our ghost tours, but what if it's true? What if Augustus isn't himself?"

Voodoo lowered the letter and now spoke directly to Augustus. "Mel emailed this to me only a few hours before she killed herself. I didn't see it until the next morning. Maybe if I'd seen it earlier, she'd still be alive." He swallowed hard and shook his head, stepping back to pace a few steps. "I thought she was crazy. Why would she be talking about demons and lies, and why would that drive her to suicide? But then I thought about it. Why would Sonny just give you his house? He loved this place. Why would you buy the business and give it such a stupid name, unless you were giving some sort of warning? Why would the church burn down minutes after we tell you to leave?"

Voodoo's arms and hands gestured wildly as he continued, "So I did my own research. I looked up this so-called Shax demon, learned all about how he found and stole treasure right out from under people. Kind of like how you suddenly rose to wealth and fame, huh? And I read all about the lies, getting people to believe and understand anything the demon tells them. So I started thinking: even if it was completely insane and made no sense at all, what if Mel was on to something? What if her suicide wasn't suicide at all, but something more?"

Augustus listened calmly to the rant, watching the other man pace back and forth while Silas stood in the background. Only when Voodoo stopped and stared at him expectantly did Augustus finally speak. "Yes?"

"Answer the fucking question."

"There were many questions. Which would you prefer I answer?"

"Who are you?" Silas asked for Voodoo, who was so furious his face had turned red.

"I am Augustus Jones." It was the truth, partially anyway.

Voodoo snarled and stomped forward. "The real Augustus doesn't talk like that, with that stupid accent, unless tourists are around. Are you really Augustus Jones, or are you a demon who took him over?"

Now Augustus paused, his façade of control threatening to slip. He didn't want to answer, but he was forced to obey his commander, and his commander wanted the truth. "I am the one they call Shax, high duke of Hell, commander of the thirty legions. I am Augustus Jones."

Both Voodoo and Silas paled. "Shit," the dreadlocked guide whispered in awe and dread, just as Voodoo pressed, "Did Mel really kill herself?"

"Yes."

"Why?"

"Because the legion told her to." At the man's frown, Augustus added, "I ordered my legion to cleanse the city of the non-believers, those who would question my reign. She was one of those non-believers. She would have threatened my rise to power, as would the twenty-nine others, and so they were taken care of."

Tears welled in Voodoo's eyes despite the rage already swimming in them. The reaction prompted interest in Augustus, who wondered if there had been more than simple platonic feelings for the woman.

"How...." His question trailed into a whisper, cut off by a catch in his voice. Clearing his throat, Voodoo tried again, "How do we get the real Augustus back, and send you back to Hell where you belong?"

"You don't." The reply was matter of fact, and the shocked silence from his captures gave Augustus time to expand. "I am not a spirit to be banished back to Hell. I am a *commander* of Hell, a servant to the Great One. You will not frighten me with idle threats. Nor will you get back the friend lost to my influence. I offered your Augustus Jones the opportunity to exist together, a symbiotic relationship where we both flourish and prosper. He instead chose insanity, the fracturing of his mind piece by piece so I was able to take him over completely."

His eyes focused on Voodoo. "The man you knew has passed into oblivion. *I* am Augustus Jones."

Quiet filled the room, disturbed only by the heavy breathing of uneasy men. Augustus shifted his glare between the two captors, one of whom was full of rage and determination, the other unsure and looking toward the door as though he wanted nothing more than to flee the house.

The smart one, he thought with an inward grin. *And, yet, the one who will suffer the most.*

"Fine," Voodoo finally spat out. "If Augustus really is gone, and no amount of rituals will get him back, then there's no reason to keep you around."

When the man brandished a gun that had formerly been tucked into the waistband at his back, Augustus felt his first inkling of fear. The demon itself couldn't be killed, but this body could, and should the body fail, the Shax would be sent back to its prison within the Will O'Wisp. It couldn't handle another century waiting for the right lost soul to succumb to the bid.

"Now we're getting somewhere." Voodoo smiled a nasty smile, one filled with the promise of death. "If Augustus is in there somewhere, tell him we're sorry, but that this had to be done."

He lifted the gun, aiming directly at Augustus's heart.

"What's going on in here?"

All three men jumped and turned to the doorway, where Gert

stood with her arms crossed and a look of horror on her face. Voodoo lowered his arm quickly, but not before she saw what he was holding. Fearlessly, she entered the room and approached her son. "What is the meaning of this? Why are you threatening to harm my son?"

"This isn't your son, ma'am," Silas said, surprising them all by speaking up. "This isn't Augustus."

"Of course not," she replied with a huff. "This is Nathaniel. My son."

Augustus looked down at the woman, brow furrowed. Mere seconds passed as he searched his brain for the name, for reasons why she would call him that, and then it clicked. The doctor saying she was losing her mind. All the times the real Augustus had to calm his confused mother. The harsh truth about her fragile mental condition.

And how he could use it to benefit him.

"This isn't your son, Ms. Jones," Voodoo said just as Augustus pleaded in his best son-like tone, carefully choosing his words, "You must help me, Mother. They are trying to hurt me."

"This isn't Augustus," Voodoo said before Gert could reply. "He's a goddamn demon possessing your son!"

The elderly woman looked at the three men in turn, ending on her son. "Nathaniel? Who are these people? Why are they saying such awful things about you?"

"They're crazy, Mother. They broke in and want to steal from us. You have to help me by moving that stick." He pointed to one of the pieces of wood by his right foot.

"Don't do it!" Voodoo shouted, lifting the gun again. Gert froze in place. "You think I won't shoot you in front of her?"

"I believe you would," Augustus replied smoothly. "But I don't believe you would shoot her, or your friend, just to eliminate the witnesses. Nor do I believe your friend would keep the secret of the murder you committed, should he be questioned."

Voodoo stole a glance over at Silas, who had paled. Neither could argue the truth in the demon's statement. The gun lowered, though Voodoo's voice was steady when growled, "You won't escape."

"This is ridiculous." Gert placed a hand on Augustus's shoulder for support, then kicked one piece of wood to the sound of Voodoo's shout.

But it was too late. The triangle was broken, and, with it, the enchantment on the demon's power. Before his captors could react, their sight was stolen from them, sending them both into black blindness. Next he took their hearing, so they were unable to help one another, let alone themselves.

In one swift move Augustus left the triangle and ripped the gun out of Voodoo's hands. The threats vanquished, he turned to Gert, whose eyes were wide and afraid. "It's okay, Mother," he told her calmly. "I'm sorry you had to see that. We were discussing business and had an idea for a new kind of show, where we talk about demons and have a role play on how to send them back to Hell. Right now my colleagues are demonstrating what a demon could do if he were to possess someone. It's quite an act, isn't it?"

Gert moved her attention to the two men crawling around the floor, searching for one another, clawing at their faces and ears, crying out in fear, stumbling into walls and furniture. "It's quite loud, Nathaniel." But she was smiling when she looked back up at him. "You and your plays and ideas. You always were such a good actor. I think your new show will be wonderful."

"Thank you." He slid an arm around her back and led her to the door. "We're going to get back to practicing. Weren't you saying you wanted to take a nap?"

After a moment's hesitation, Gert nodded. "Yes. A nap sounds nice. Have fun, Nathaniel."

Then she left the demon to its victims.

CHAPTER 32

Only when the old woman had left the room and retreated to her bedroom did Augustus turn back to the men still stumbling their way around. It would have been comical, if not for what was about to happen.

Before tending to the men, Augustus perused the room, stepping around Silas, who was clinging to the coffee table and furiously wiping at his eyes in a worthless attempt to regain his sight. He found what he was looking for above the fireplace mantle: a Civil War-era blade encased in glass.

Pulling the box down from its hooks, Augustus retrieved the knife and nodded to himself. "Yes," he muttered. "This will do quite nicely."

Ready to resume, he pulled in a deep breath, and with it gave back the sight and hearing of his victims while taking away something else—control over their limbs. They could do nothing but slump to the floor, Voodoo propped up by the couch and Silas on his back.

"Pride has always been the downfall of your kind," Augustus began, hands behind his back to hide the weapon he now held. "You think you have all the answers, that you can solve any problem. You think you deserve more, that the world owes you more. Your pride makes you vulnerable. It makes you easy to manipulate."

A chuckle escaped when Voodoo made to reply, but only dry air croaked from his throat.

"Oh, I suppose I should explain. Your research must have failed you to the whole of who I am." He lowered himself to Voodoo's level. "I can take from you your sight, your hearing, your ability to speak, even your ability to move. Because that is what I do. I deceive, and I have the power to make even your own body deceive itself."

Straightening, Augustus moved to Silas and grabbed the man by the ankle, dragging him to the center of the room. The younger man could only manage a terrified whimper. Once he had positioned his victim, Augustus set his sights on Voodoo, rearranging the man to give him an unobstructed view.

"Augustus Jones was a good guide to his people," he said casually. "I wonder if he knew just how much truth there was to his stories."

He turned and paced around the room, looking at all the decorations of his new home, prolonging their fear. "I'm sure you're wondering which stories have truths to them," he said to Voodoo, all but ignoring Silas. "The answer is many of them, but today, let's discuss just one."

Showing Voodoo the knife, enjoying the way his eyes widened and his mouth moved to say something, perhaps beg for mercy. Augustus stopped at Silas's feet. "Rituals are a powerful thing. They can summon the darkest of spirits, force demons to confess to their deepest secrets, and even give greater life to the commander. An evocation, if you will."

Lowering himself, Augustus straddled Silas's stomach and sat on his knees. He used the knife to cut the man's shirt in half up the center, then cocked his head to the side, taking in the intricate design tattooed up the man's ribcage. Using the tip of the knife, he traced one black spiral from naval to pectoral, leaving behind a thin scratch of flesh.

"Augustus told his followers stories of rituals," he said with a sideways look at Voodoo. "That when you consume a person's heart, so too do you consume their power. Do you know what this means?"

Realization dawned on Voodoo in a panic seen only in the wild glimmer of his dark eyes. Augustus could see the strain in his every nerve, in the way his veins popped and face reddened. He was fighting the spell against him, and losing.

"Ah, so you see where this ritual is going, do you?" The tip of the knife stopped at Silas's heart. The trapped man's eyes were wide, tears spilling from the corners and dripping to the hardwood floor. He, too, knew what was soon to happen, and couldn't stop his imminent death.

"Did you know," Augustus continued, crooning to them both, "that power comes in many forms? Your kind does not hold the sort of power mine does, but, rather, something different." The knife pressed down lightly, enough to spill the first drop of blood. "Your kind has youth, understanding of the world in which you live, innovative ideas, ambition to transform the world around you. The kind of power I will need to survive as the famous Augustus Jones."

Voodoo's lips parted in a silent scream, his body jerking with the effort. The scream formed his friend's name, just as the knife slid down, through flesh, between bone.

"I am sorry for this, old friend," Augustus said down to Silas. The man's face was nearly purple, eyes bulged out, mouth gasping for air and throat tight with unheard pleas for help. The pain was visible in his expression, in the way his eyes squeezed shut only to flutter open with fresh tear. The demon really wasn't one to enjoy the way bodies writhed in pain; that was for the Asag, the spirit it had been trapped with for far too long, forced to hear stories of death and despair.

"It will be over soon," he promised, cutting deeper, not letting himself look at Silas's face, lest he lose the bloodlust needed to complete the job. Blood had started to ooze from the corners of his victim's mouth, bubbling up with each cough and gasp. His breath rattled from his chest, which now held a six-inch-long lesion.

"Soon," Augustus whispered again, sliding his fingers into the wound, grasping ribs and muscle and tendon on either side of the chest cavity. Then, with a deep breath, he yanked with all his might.

Cracking bone and tearing flesh sounded in the air. It took but seconds for the final breath to shudder out of Silas's torn chest, just as Voodoo gagged and vomited upon himself, closing his eyes against the sight of his friend literally torn apart.

Augustus didn't notice any of it. He saw what he wanted, needed—the man's heart, beating its final beat. With a grim smile, he reached down and tugged the organ free from its constraints. He remained sitting upon the still body and used the knife to slice off a piece of the heart, placing it tenderly on his tongue and savoring the tangy taste of blood and muscle.

Piece by piece, he consumed Silas's heart, with every swallow feeling more invigorated, more knowledgeable, completely revitalized. Only when his hand was empty did he moved from his hunched-over position, stretching his back and cracking his neck, before turning to Voodoo.

The other man's cheeks were stained with tears, shirt covered in drying vomit, eyes bloodshot. He was trying to look away from the disturbing sight in front of him, but every so often his gaze trailed back, perhaps hoping to see something different, to see it was all just a nightmare and he'd finally woken up.

Rising, Augustus licked his lips and sucked the blood from his thumb, not noticing how stained his clothes were. He sauntered over to Voodoo and knelt next to him. "Do you know why I chose you?" he asked softly, lifting one of Voodoo's arms. "I chose you to live, and the other to die. But do you know why?"

Augustus placed the knife in Voodoo's hands, wrapping his fingers around the hilt. The man's body responded to the silent command, gripping the blade firmly. "You are insignificant to this story," he told Voodoo. "You are but a peasant to the royalty, and when the peasants revolt, it is they who suffer, not the king."

With careful moves, Augustus lifted a hand and smeared what was left of the blood on his fingers across Voodoo's face. When he needed more, he walked back and forth from body to body, gathering blood and coating Voodoo around the mouth, then on his hands and wrists. When he was done, the ghost tour guide looked every bit the part of crazed, heart-eating killer.

Augustus sat back on his heels to observe his work. "Nicely done," he told himself, then looked down. "This won't do. Please excuse me." Making quick work of his cleanup, Augustus cleansed his skin of blood and changed into a fresh set of clothes, storing the soiled shirt and pants in a tightly sealed bag he shoved beneath his bed. He would deal with the burning of those garments later.

Once he was clean, he picked up the phone in his room and made a single call, then returned to the living room, finding the men exactly where he'd left them. "Now," he said to Voodoo through narrowed eyes, "it's time for you to learn what you've done."

Voodoo's brow furrowed and it looked like he wanted to protest, but he couldn't stop what would happen next.

"How could you, Voodoo?" Augustus asked, his voice sounding more human in this moment than ever before. "You murdered Silas, your best friend, all for a ritual you knew, deep down, would never work. I understand that you loved Mel and wanted her back, and that you would do anything to have her in your arms, but this was not the answer. You looked up ritual after ritual, searching for a way to bring her back to life, and finally found one that required a human sacrifice. You had to kill someone special to you, a close friend or family member, and consume their heart in order to have the power to raise the dead. Except, it didn't work."

He paused, letting the first part of his lie sink in. His human brain could see the event that never happened as it might have occurred—how Voodoo would see it as fact.

"So you lured Silas here, planning to frame me out of jealousy for my relationship with Mel. But after killing Silas and eating his heart, and realizing the ritual didn't work, you became consumed with guilt. How could you have done this? you asked yourself. How could you have killed Silas, who was such a good man? You have genuinely lost your mind, Voodoo, and now all you want to do is confess to what you've done."

Sirens blared in the distance. Augustus lifted his head to listen, then looked back at Voodoo, who was sitting silently with fresh tears sliding down his cheeks, mixing with the blood caked around his mouth. The gears of his brain were shifting and turning, confining to the new reality in which he killed Silas, he ate a man's heart, he murdered an innocent man out of love.

"They're coming for you," he said quietly. "It's time you confess to your sins, Voodoo. It will all be over soon."

Rising, Augustus sighed and lifted a hand. The single motion gave Voodoo back his faculties, though he didn't use them. The man merely hunched over and sobbed, bloody hands covering an even bloodier face.

Augustus turned his back to the carnage and walked to the front door. He would meet the police with a grim expression, full of apology and panic, and he would see to it his lie was met by all of Savannah with sympathy and regret.

And then, when his enemies were effectively eliminated, he would resume his new life as Augustus Jones.

CHAPTER 33

He stood in the expansive backyard, hands in his pockets, looking down the hill at the enormous, crystalline pool. Gert was there, lying back in a chair beneath the bright sun with a blanket wrapped tightly around her shoulders, two elderly women on either side of her, and they were laughing.

It was a good day, one where his mother was happy, in her right mind, no longer worrying what the news said or if anyone would want to talk to her about the horrible event her house had seen. Augustus had shielded her from it all over the past few months, dealing with the press and police himself, until the hype finally died down.

But with the hype came business, more than expected. His name had been cleared of any wrongdoing, yet the notoriety that was earned by being connected to such a grisly murder had brought in tourists by the droves. He'd hired four guides, two from competing companies, and already was sold out for tours for the next four months.

"Life is good," he said with confidence, turning back toward the house. That confidence waned when he looked up at the enormous home, surrounded by landscaped gardens and structures. An old worry of his mother's came to mind—how would he afford all of this?

The demon had learned a lot of Augustus Jones lately, and a lot of how the world's finances worked. There was not enough money to cover the expenses in the man's measly bank account, or prospective business fortune.

But he knew where to find what he needed.

Augustus Jones was a great storyteller in his time. He had known how to weave words in a way that captivated his audience. And, unbeknownst to him, his very first lie after the bid had been won, had been the lie that would benefit the demon the most.

Leaving his mother to her friends—friends she'd met after he encouraged her to leave the house more and join a local seniors' club—Augustus headed back inside for the car keys, then peeled out of the circular driveway and headed back toward the heart of town.

Tourist season was long over, and with the bitter cold in the air, few people were out in the city. But it made no difference to Augustus. When he reached his destination, he would clear the area by his influence alone. Those who managed to sneak past would be taken care of by his legion of loyal followers.

Calhoun Square was empty when he stepped off the sidewalk and onto the grass. The sun was just starting to lower, sending long shadows across the small park that helped cloak him in darkness. Looking down, he imagined the stories Augustus used to tell of slaves buried beneath the square.

"Not today, friends," he said down at the earth. "But, someday, you shall be needed."

Augustus had his followers, the ones he needed to complete today's task. Leaving the square, he crossed the street and found his destination: the old Espy house, where one Carl Espy once lived and breathed and squirreled away an alleged fortune. A fortune completely made up by Augustus for fun.

The tour guide hadn't realized at the time what his lie would do—recreate history and alter the life of a man long since dead. And, more importantly, set the stage for a grand fortune to be discovered.

Tipping his head back, Augustus called to his loyal legion, enjoying the familiar rumbling of the earth and sound of hooves on asphalt. Within moments thirty cloaked men on black horses surrounded him. They would be invisible to any mortal who passed, though they would feel a cold wind shiver up their spine, maybe hear a whispered warning in their ear to make them hurry home and lock the door behind them.

"Evening, my legion. It has been far too long since I have had the honor to call upon you," Augustus began, turning a circle to address them all. "I thank you for your service to my former host. He knew not what he did, but you followed him well, and will be rewarded for your service."

The men nodded in response, always silent until called upon to speak. They sat stoically upon their horses, some clutching the hilts of swords, others holding tight to the reins.

"Half of you will guard this square. Keep everyone off the streets in the surrounding area, and let no one in or out. The other half will come with me on foot. Divide yourselves, and make haste."

A sense of power filled Augustus. It had been so long since he'd been in command of his legion, and he'd forgotten how much he loved it, how strong and invincible it made him feel to be in charge of Hell's best warriors.

The legion made quick work of dividing themselves, fifteen men dropping from horseback and standing in three straight rows five deep before him, swords at the ready. The other half spread out to begin their patrols.

Augustus nodded at the ones on foot. "You are good men to follow me into battle. Except, this will not be a battle, so you need not worry about weapons." As expected, they sheathed their swords. "Follow me."

With a brisk and determined walk, Augustus followed the path in his mind's eye to the old house the former ghost tour guide had once explained as belonging to a judge-turned-bootlegger. Those same memories told him the house was empty. No one would live there because of the alleged paranormal activity that scared former residents away, and so the property was kept up by the city as a historical landmark.

"Today, history redeems itself," Augustus announced, and shoved open the front door.

Here, his memories couldn't help him. The real Augustus Jones had never been in the house. But the demon understood enough of the home to know what to look for, and so he opened every door on the first floor until he found the one with a flight of stairs leading down.

"Follow me," he said again to the legion, and together they marched down the stairs in a line. Once they had all huddled in the basement, a small and unfinished room that reeked of mold and old water, he looked at his men. "We are looking for a secret room. A tunnel, a passageway, something secluded and hidden that will open up into a new room. Find it."

They broke apart to search individually, tearing through years' worth of junk that was better suited for the garbage. Several soldiers felt around the floor, turning over shelves and furniture and boxes of random items in hopes of finding a trapdoor. The others, Augustus included, went for the walls, feeling for creases that would indicate a hidden passage.

Then it hit him—this was Augustus Jones's story. It had no real truth, and as such was easily molded to suit his needs. The demon had to laugh at his own foolishness, and was about to weave a tale where a door would easily be found, when one of his soldiers beckoned from his left.

Augustus rushed to the legionnaire and, together with four others, they pried open a hidden doorway tucked behind a bookcase. It was a small door, barely noticeable save for the rusted latch. They dug their fingers into the creases, pulling out crumbles of wood and dirt, then tugged the door open, a rush of stale air their first greeting.

"Follow me." The repeated command was the only thing he said to the soldiers as he dropped to his knees and crawled through the door, using the flashlight he'd brought for just this occasion to light the way. The legionnaires didn't need a light; darkness would be no different than the morning sun to them.

It was a short crawl through the earth before the walls opened up. Augustus finished his crawl until he could stand, shining the light around the square room, not surprised to find it empty. According to the original lie, this room had already been discovered and cleaned out. But, as legend told, there was another room with even greater treasure.

The search began again, and it was a quick one. Augustus discovered the hidden hatch behind an empty chest. Sucking in a deep breath, he dared to enter the shaft, not frightened by the darkness or cramped quarters, eager to see what awaited him on the other side. It was a short crawl, no more than five or six feet, before he was nearly dropped into the second hidden room. Here he could smell wet earth and wood rot, but also the distinct scent of metal.

"Let there be light," Augustus said with a chuckle, and shined the flashlight in the room.

Gold glinted back at him. And, not just gold, but blues and reds and greens of precious gemstones of all sizes. There was no organization to the room, just stacks of wooden chests, threadbare bags tied around heaps of gold coins, piles of gold bars hidden behind heaps of loose diamonds. So much treasure, he couldn't take it all in at once.

"Gentlemen," Augustus said to his soldiers, not able to help the genuine smile that crossed his face, "this is the fortune to free us all."

With a laugh, he dipped his hand in a pile of coins, marveling at the sound they made. He picked up an emerald as large as his hand, knowing from centuries of experience it was real, and very, very expensive.

"Remove every last piece," he ordered the men, pocketing the emerald, "and take it to my home. Stack it neatly in the building shaped like a temple in the back corner. You will know the building I mean." He'd discovered it just that morning, a shrine-like structure he guessed was used for meditation or prayer. Now it would be the temporary hiding place for his fortune.

"And then, my loyal legion, you all will be rewarded."

He left his soldiers to their task, crawling out of the hidden rooms and surfacing outside, where night had long since fallen. The other legionnaires roamed about, protecting the property from prying eyes. Leaving them to their patrol, Augustus left the house, pride, satisfaction, and power humming in his chest.

His feet took him to the house that had once been his prison. Never before had he seen it through his own eyes from the outside. Once it had been a place of torture, where insanity was always a moment away, and hope was but a call to the darkness as they waited for a fool to enter. Now he was free, free to live the life of Augustus Jones, and, when this body was about to expire, find a new host. There were always liars, those who wanted more, who thought they deserved more.

This world was his for the taking.

"Worry not, Tisiphone," the Shax said to the last remaining spirit trapped within those walls, with only the Will O'Wisp for company. "Your time will come."

Then he nodded once toward the house, a simple sign of respect for the only company he'd had in centuries, and turned away. The house on Abercorn was no longer a concern. He was freed by a man whose lies were too large to bear, but that created a world ripe for the demon's picking.

Now he would live in those lies. He would run a business more successful than any before. He would live in a home fit for a king. He would charm women with his good looks and charisma, and bask in the glow of a golden fortune. And, above all, he would take over the world one mistruth at a time.

He was, after all, Augustus Jones. And nothing could touch him now.

EPILOGUE

The Will O'Wisp watched from the front window as the man it once knew as Augustus Jones stared up from the sidewalk. It knew who, or what, was watching, could see not the influence of a demon at work, but a whole-body takeover.

Augustus was gone, in mind and soul but not in body. The Shax had consumed the unsuspecting man completely, leaving behind nothing but a familiar face to trick the rest of the world. A sad ending for a good man, the Will O'Wisp considered, but not a surprising one. It had seen many men like Augustus Jones, the ones who wanted too much and believed themselves to be greater than what they were. Those men always fell, and there were always more to take their place.

The new Augustus spoke directly to the single demon left, causing the light to blaze and lick the ceiling, leaving behind a black mark to signify its rage. *Your time will come*, the Will O'Wisp repeated the Shax's promise, spoken on a smooth Irish lilt, hoping both, this time, spoke the truth. Only one was left, and the bid would have to be with the perfect soul.

From the sidewalk, Augustus nodded. The Will O'Wisp accepted the gesture as a symbol of respect and returned it, then backed away from the window as the man on the other side of the glass walked away as well. There were no ill feelings between them—they'd both been trapped here, and the Will O'Wisp was happy for the spirit's freedom.

Before tucking itself back into the shadows to sleep away the gloom of another night's imprisonment, the Will O'Wisp took a glimpse into its inner vision to check on the girl. Two had entered the house the night Augustus Jones was taken over, and two had left with demons to follow them home.

It saw her now, the teenage girl plagued by nightmares, confused and scared but also thrilled by the new powers granted to her by a demon whispering in her ear. Already there was so much carnage, endless destruction, all at the hands of a girl who knew not what she did.

The Will O'Wisp shut off its vision, not wanting to see more. It knew what would happen, what always happened. Just like the others, the girl would fall.

And, when she did, her entire world would crumble.

ABOUT THE AUTHOR

Night owl, Dorito lover, and quiet eccentric—Kristina Circelli is the author of several fiction novels that span genres, including *The Helping Hands* series, *The Whisper Legacy*, *Fragile Creatures*, *Damsel Not*, and *The Never*.

A follower of her Cherokee heritage, self-professed movie addict, and potential crazy cat lady, Circelli holds both a Bachelor of Arts and Master of Arts in English from the University of North Florida. She also heads Red Road Editing, a full-service editing company for independent authors. Her popular cultural novel Beyond the Western Sun is taught in middle schools, where she frequently offers talks and workshops for aspiring young writers.

She currently resides in Florida with her husband, Seth; cats, Lord Finnegin the Fierce and Master Malachi the Mighty; and dachshund, Pippin the Powerful. (Though she has not-so-secret covert plans to move everyone to New Zealand some day.)

BOOK

PERMUTED PRESS
needs **you** to help

SPREAD INFECTION

FOLLOW US!

f | Facebook.com/PermutedPress
🐦 | Twitter.com/PermutedPress

REVIEW US!

Wherever you buy our book, they can be reviewed! We want to know what you like!

GET INFECTED!

Sign up for our mailing list at
PermutedPress.com

PERMUTED
PRESS

14

Peter Clines

Padlocked doors. Strange light fixtures. Mutant cockroaches.

There are some odd things about Nate's new apartment. Every room in this old brownstone has a mystery. Mysteries that stretch back over a hundred years. Some of them are in plain sight. Some are behind locked doors. And all together these mysteries could mean the end of Nate and his friends.

Or the end of everything...

PERMUTED
PRESS

THE JOURNAL SERIES
by Deborah D. Moore

After a major crisis rocks the nation, all supply lines are shut down. In the remote Upper Peninsula of Michigan, the small town of Moose Creek and its residents are devastated when they lose power in the middle of a brutal winter, and must struggle alone with one calamity after another.

The Journal series takes the reader head first into the fury that only Mother Nature can dish out.

THE BREADWINNER | Stevie Kopas

The end of the world is not glamorous. In a matter of days the human race was reduced to nothing more than vicious, flesh hungry creatures. There are no heroes here. Only survivors. The trilogy continues with Book Two: *Haven* and Book Three: *All Good Things*.

THE BECOMING | Jessica Meigs

As society rapidly crumbles under the hordes of infected, three people—Ethan Bennett, a Memphis police officer; Cade Alton, his best friend and former IDF sharpshooter; and Brandt Evans, a lieutenant in the US Marines—band together against the oncoming crush of death and terror sweeping across the world. The story continues with Book Two: *Ground Zero*.

THE INFECTION WAR | Craig DiLouie

As the undead awake, a small group of survivors must accept a dangerous mission into the very heart of infection. This edition features two books: *The Infection* and *The Killing Floor*.

OBJECTS OF WRATH | Sean T. Smith

The border between good and evil has always been bloody... Is humanity doomed? After the bombs rain down, the entire world is an open wound; it is in those bleeding years that William Fox becomes a man. After The Fall, nothing is certain. *Objects of Wrath* is the first book in a saga spanning four generations.

PERMUTED
PRESS